PEYTON BANKS

"Wade Brooks, how the hell are ya?"

Grinning, Wade walked forward and shook the well-respected rancher's hand. "I'm doing well, Mr. Bowman. How's the wife?"

Mr. Bowman laughed. He was a boisterous man whose ranch was located on the other side of Shady Springs. "Still driving me crazy, but she ain't driven me into the ground yet."

He patted the man on the back. "You two will be fine. It's good to see ya, Mr. Bowman."

After the old man nodded and walked away, Wade blew out a deep breath and looked around the farm, bustling with people from far and wide who had come for the auction.

Shifting the baseball cap on his head, he continued to stroll the grounds. The sun was high, and already the temperature was climbing. It was a perfect day for the event, even though it was a somber one. No man wanted to be in the Roman family's shoes. They'd been hit with hard times, and from what Wade had heard, they owed Uncle Sam a pretty hefty sum. The auction was one way to keep from selling their entire farm to pay the taxman. Horses, machinery, and even antiques were said to be up for bidding.

Wade was interested in the horses, but was open to see all they would have available.

Depending on the amount they owed, the land would be next.

Arriving at the corral, he leaned against the fence where the horses were being kept for bidders to observe before they went up for sale, eyeing a few potentials.

The Brookses, Wade's family, was well known in the county and legendary in the state, owning and operating the Blazing Eagle Ranch, the largest cattle ranch in Colorado. Wade was a fourth-generation rancher who would one day share the full responsibility of running it with his brothers.

He was extremely close with his brothers, Parker and Carson. Parker, the eldest, had been a bull rider at the top of his game, until an injury ended his career. Returning home to the family ranch, he dove into his responsibilities as a Brooks man. Their younger brother, Carson, had gone off to play college football.

After receiving his degree, he then came back to work alongside Wade and their father, Jonah.

Wade had held the ranch down while his brothers were off pursuing their dreams. Attending junior college online, he got a degree in business. His heart had been on the ranch. The open skies and the land were his bloodline, and he had worked his fingers to the bone to help ensure Blazing Eagle prospered.

He had founded The Kiddie Camp, something he loved. It gave him a chance to work with the youth and help cultivate future ranchers and farmers. Every summer, Blazing Eagle was overrun with children of all ages who wanted to learn the ins and outs of ranching. He had a solid crew who taught the kids how to ride horses, organized activities, and even hosted a camping trip.

Kiddie Camp was very popular and expanded every year.

His nephew, Tyler, thrived on it. He was a fantastic kid who Wade enjoyed spending time with. He was proud Parker had finally met his son. It had been a hard pill to swallow to learn of the depths their father had gone through to keep Parker away from Maddy.

Jonah was a hardened man who always preached that Brooks men should look after each other. Welp,

Jonah had done the unthinkable by lying to keep Parker and Maddy apart. Little did he, or any of them know, Maddy was pregnant when she disappeared.

When she'd reappeared, all hell had broken loose, and all the lies were brought to light.

Luckily for Parker, he and Maddy got their happy ending. They were now engaged and expecting again.

Wade shook his head, trying to concentrate on a particular horse who stood out, away from the others, staring right at him.

This one had spunk and attitude.

Jonah had taught him and his brothers all they needed to know about the family business. As the next generation to take over the ranch, Jonah was insistent upon the boys inheriting Blazing Eagle, settling down, and raising families of their own.

Wade snorted.

It wasn't that he was opposed to settling down; it was just the opposite. He was thirty years old and realized it was time to find that special someone.

But that was the problem.

Where would he find her?

"Well, well, well. Looks like the vultures are hovering."

Wade stiffened as Joy Whitaker leaned against the fence next to him.

He wasn't going to counter with a snide remark.

Joy always tried to get under his skin, and her comment was a spiteful dig on his family crest, which was that of an eagle, hence the Blazing Eagle Ranch. But he wasn't going to correct her.

There had been bad blood between their families long before either of them were born. It was practically a custom for a Brooks not to get along with a Whitaker.

He'd known Joy since they were kids, and she was a fierce competitor in everything she did, from perfect grades in school, to racing horses, and even horseshoes.

But there was something else about her.

She was a beauty.

Light brown skin, dark brown hair with blonde highlights, and light, hazel eyes, that at the moment were reflecting the sun, appearing almost amber.

Her curves were what every man dreamed of, so it was a wonder she wasn't already tied down and starting a family of her own. All the eligible men in town pined after her, but none were courageous enough to approach the little spitfire.

Wade sighed, turning his attention back to the horses when someone added a few sheep to the corral. "What do you want, Joy?"

"Wondering what you're doing here. Doesn't the Blazing Eagle have enough horses?" She turned her killer smile on him and inclined slightly toward him.

When he caught the scent of her floral perfume, he

shook his head. "We do, but I run a camp, and I'm always searching for the best horses to train for the kids. If a fellow rancher needs to liquidate their assets, I would be willing to offer them a fair price."

He didn't have to offer her an explanation, but the way she watched him put him on the defensive.

How the hell did she rile him the way she did?

"Your family sure seems to make a habit out of trying to help others by buying their assets."

Wade's cheeks warmed. He swung around and glared at her, knowing exactly what she was hinting at. Years ago, before either of them were born, his grandfather, Cyrus Brooks, had made a deal with Macon Whitaker, Joy's grandfather. The Whitakers had come upon hard times themselves, and Cyrus purchased land from Macon to help them out, and allow them to get their hands on some much-needed cash.

The Whitakers had never let them live it down.

Because of a deal gone wrong, there had been bad blood between their families ever since. He Wade had never wanted any part of it, and had nothing to do with it, but because of his last name, he was the enemy of any Whitaker who lived in Shady Springs.

Joy returned his glare and stood with her hand on her hip. She tossed her long, dark hair over her shoulder, as if to dare him to argue with her.

Joy Whitaker lived to argue with him.

He wasn't going to play into her little game today, though.

"The Blazing Eagle isn't selling any land no time soon." Wade smirked. That would rattle her something fierce.

Joy narrowed her gaze on him. It had worked.

If smoke could come out of her ears, it would. Wade loved seeing her pissed off. Her brown eyes darkened, and her nose flared. She was downright cute when she was pissed off.

"That piece of land your house sits on used to be Whitaker land," she bit out through clenched teeth, her hands balled into tiny fists.

"Keyword is *used* to be," he taunted.

Growling, she spun away on her heels and marched off without glancing back at Wade. His gaze strayed down to her nice round ass as he took notice of her swaying hips.

His cock took notice too.

What the hell was he doing? If she knew he was checking her out, she'd more than likely turn her shears on him, shaving him like she would the sheep her family raised.

Wade's gaze followed her until she disappeared through the thick crowd.

Shaking his head, he pushed back off the fence and moved on. He had to get her off his mind. Turning his focus back to the reason he was at the auction, he thrust all thoughts of how sexy Joy Whitaker was when she was mad at him out of his head.

The auction should be starting soon, and he wanted to see what else would be up for purchase. He wasn't sure what he was there for, but he was an honest businessman, and if he saw a deal, he'd make an offer.

Walking through the large barn, he inspected some tractors that appeared to be in good shape. A few other men gathered around the machines, checking them out as well.

Strolling over to the hood of one, he hefted it up, leaned over it, and assessed the dirty metal. The engine looked sturdy. He wasn't an expert, but he was sure Carson could give it a good tune-up. He loved to tinker in the garage, and this would be the perfect project for his younger brother.

"Fine machine, huh?" a gravelly voice spoke up next to Wade.

Lifting his head, he met the gaze of an older gentleman in a black and gray plaid shirt, jeans, and a wide-brimmed hat. His face was covered in wrinkles, which easily spoke of a man who'd spent most of his life out in the sun.

Wade nodded. "Seems to be good."

"I hear it runs pretty decent, but needs a good fixin'. You thinking of making a bid?"

Wade stepped back and wiped his hands on his jeans. He didn't want to give away if he was or wasn't. Reaching up, he closed the hood as softly as he could.

"Doubt it. I was just browsing." It was well-known that at auctions, these such people lingered around to get a feel of what would be popular so the price could be driven up. Giving the stranger a nod, he walked away.

Wade wandered around a bit more, taking in other things marked for sale. The hairs on the back of his neck suddenly rose.

Someone was watching him.

Casually, he glanced about. The barn was full of people taking in the inventory that would soon be auctioned off. And then, his eyes met a pair of familiar brown ones.

Joy.

Enjoying the fact that he rattled her, he grinned wide, tipping his hat to her. She crossed her arms and rolled her eyes before ambling around the barn.

"The auction will be starting in five minutes," a voice announced over the speakers. "Five minutes until the auction begins!"

The crowd shifted and headed toward the auction

block out in the back. Wade followed, having made up his mind about a few things he'd bid on.

It was a beautiful day outside. The skies were clear, and the atmosphere was light. There was nothing like a good ol' country auction.

"Who the hell does Wade Brooks think he is?" Joy grumbled as she stalked toward her pickup truck, still fuming. The day had been going quite well until she'd laid eyes on the tall rancher. Yanking open the driver's side door, she jumped behind the wheel and slammed the door shut. Sitting back, she attempted to calm herself down.

That man sure had a way of pissing her off.

And with only a smile at that.

Just because he had money and wealth, didn't mean he needed to flaunt it.

"If a fellow rancher needs to liquidate their assets, then I would be willing to offer them a fair price."

Talk about arrogant and privileged.

Like his money would save the poor family who'd been hit with hard times.

Her stomach clenched at that country drawl of his. Why did she have to react to him the way she did? Just the sound of his voice sent a ripple of chills down her spine. It was deep and smooth. That slight twang in his accent was downright sexy.

Wade had been a thorn in her side since high school, with he and his brothers always the talk of the town. They had played varsity football. The youngest, Carson, was the only one who went away to play at the college level.

She had been a volleyball player and was naturally competitive. Her senior year, her team had even won the state championship.

But girls' volleyball didn't have the draw the Wade brothers and Shady Springs high school football did. The male sports players were treated like superstars around town, while the girls were treated like second-class citizens.

Not that she was still stuck in high school or anything, but twelve years after graduation, it still left a bad taste in her mouth. Though, it wasn't just that.

The Whitakers and Brookses had bad blood between them, the rivalry dating back to before she was born. Jonah Brooks drove a wedge between the two neighboring families. It was something she had heard about her entire life from her father.

A man with the last name of Brooks wasn't to be trusted.

Joy started her truck and drove down the winding road of the farm toward the main highway.

The farther away she got from Wade Brooks, the more it seemed her blood pressure decreased. Gunning the engine, she headed into town.

Shady Springs was a pleasant area to grow up in. She had lived there her entire life, and couldn't see herself calling any other place home. She was a small-town girl with a big heart.

Her family settled in Colorado around the mid-thirties. Her grandparents had migrated from a town in Alabama and set out to follow their dreams of purchasing land to own and cultivate. It was tough back then. A black family moving from the Deep South to the middle of the country was unheard of.

Her grandparents settled in Shady Springs during a time when there was still segregation. They were the second black family to move to the area during a time when owning a ranch or farm was predominately white. They had to worry about people hating them for the color of their skin, but the country was in the midst of the Great Depression.

But Macon and Lila Whitaker were strong, persevering when everything was against them. They moved to Colorado with the little funds they had saved up. The land was cheap, so they were able to make their purchase.

And the Fox Run Ranch was born.

During this time, Shady Springs was barely considered a town. It boasted a general store, a bar, a gas station, and that was pretty much it.

Her family had remained to see the town flourish into what it was today, and she was proud to have the last name of Whitaker.

It stood for something.

But then, hard times had fallen upon the Whitakers.

Macon struck a deal with James Brooks, who'd agreed to a land deal for the Whitakers to come into the cash needed to pay off their debts. The Whitakers were promised they would have the opportunity to purchase their land back.

Macon and James shook on the deal.

Later, the Whitakers recovered. They were once again on their feet and in the black. Things were looking good for the sheep ranchers.

Years had passed, and the new generations were running the ranches. Joy's father, Davis Sr., approached Jonah, requesting to purchase back their land. Davis was willing to pay the going price for the property at the time, but Jonah refused.

The elder Brooks would not honor the agreement that his father had gone into with Macon. It was Brookses land, and he wasn't selling it back.

The feud between them was official.

Joy had been hearing of the stories since she was knee high to a grasshopper.

Arriving into town, she made her way to the gas station. The light on her dashboard popped on, signaling she was low on fuel.

"Oh, all right. I'll fill you up now," Joy murmured. A few minutes later, she parked next to the pump and shut her engine off. Reaching over for her purse, she snatched out some cash before exiting the vehicle.

Walking around to the other side of the truck, Joy paused.

Wade was standing on the opposite side of her pump, getting gas.

What the hell?

Seeing him twice in one day was enough. She ignored the butterflies that always seemed to appear in her stomach when she was near him.

When his gaze landed on hers, his lips spread into that sexy grin of his.

"You know you didn't have to follow me, right?" he teased.

She shrugged. "I needed gas. How was I to know you would be at this gas station?" The town now had three fuel stations, and, of course, she had to pick the one he would be at.

He left his truck and stepped over to her. She was

taken aback by his size, those steel-gray eyes, and dark, curly hair.

As much as she tried to deny it, she was attracted to him.

There was no way in hell she was letting him know that, though.

"Here, I'll pump your gas for you." He grabbed the nozzle and turned to her truck.

"I can do it." She brushed his hand away from the gas lid. "I've been pumping gas since I was fourteen."

When he only stared at her, she tried not to fidget under his gaze.

"Why do you have to fight me at every turn? Why can't I just be a gentleman and pump gas for a pretty little lady?"

Her heart raced. Wade thought she was pretty? She pushed down the excitement and folded her arms.

Stepping aside, she allowed him to insert the nozzle.

"Is that how you catch them?" Joy asked. She couldn't help it. She had a smart mouth, and most times, it ran before she could stop it.

"Who?" He focused on her with his eyebrows raised.

"Women. Do they fall for the knight in shining armor complex you got going?" She pushed her hair over her shoulder and waited for his answer.

The Brooks' brothers had a way with women, as all of them were heart-stoppers. Women old and young took notice of a Brooks man when he entered a room.

Wade's deep chuckle caused a shiver to glide down her spine. His gaze roamed her body, and she fought to keep from moving. She'd dressed in a soft tee, jeans, and boots. Being a rancher's daughter, she wasn't the most feminine girl around.

Though, she did have one vice.

Sexy lingerie.

It was her little secret, and not even her mother knew about it.

Wade moved closer to her, resting against her truck. With his size, he invaded her space, but she was too stubborn to take a step back. His scent filled her nostrils, and she had to keep herself from leaning in closer to sniff him.

How dare he smell so damn good.

She had to lock her knees because they grew weak. That crooked grin of Wade's was back.

He knew what he was doing.

Lord help her.

When he ran his hand through his thick mop of curls, she might have whimpered a little.

Wade Brooks had just turned on his charm, and she was falling for it.

She now understood why all the women went

crazy over him.

"Now, see here, Joy." His voice dropped a few decibels and became husky, that drawl of his increasing. "When I have my sights on a woman, she never falls. Some begging, maybe, but she never falls. I'd catch her."

Joy paused, letting his words register.

She rolled her eyes, but couldn't stop her lips from spreading into a small smile. Wade's smile widened.

"That is so corny." She snuck a peek at the total on the pump. "I'll go pay for my gas. Thanks for pumping it. At least a Brooks is good for something." She walked away to go inside the gas station.

His comment of "some begging" took her breath away.

What exactly would she have to beg for?

Joy parked in the gravel near the main house and laughed. Stepping out of the vehicle, she was bombarded by her favorite, four-legged fur babies. Lacy, Minnie, and Duke were mutts she'd adopted at the pound who'd turned out to be great ranching dogs.

They loved working with the sheep. The spacious, open land, and being able to roam free on a ranch was great for the dogs. They all earned their keep.

The Fox Run Ranch was smaller than their neighbors at the Blazing Eagle Ranch, but Joy was proud of their stead. It was named as such because of the problem with foxes. They always snuck onto the property to steal chickens and livestock.

Her grandfather had named it so after watching the foxes that ran through the wild. When they'd purchased the land, it had been abandoned due to the dry climate. So, to give it a fresh start, Macon Whitaker renamed the property.

Fox Run was perfect.

"How're y'all doing?" Joy rubbed their heads, laughing at how excited they were acting. There was nothing better than coming home and being greeted by her own little cheering squad. Her dogs were like her children. Duke jumped up onto his hind legs so he could reach her. She laughed, giving him a hug. "Are you hungry?"

They yipped and barked as they jumped and danced around her legs.

"Okay!" Joy cried out. She pushed them away so she could walk without tripping and falling. "Let's go get something to eat."

The dogs took off toward the barn as if the gates of Hell had opened. They paused halfway and turned to check that she was behind them.

Minnie barked as if to tell Joy to hurry.

"I'm coming."

She walked into the barn behind the dogs, who were leading the way. The crazy mutts ran over to where their bowls were kept and picked them up in their mouths.

She couldn't help but laugh at their antics.

She hurried over and took care of them, ensuring their bowls were full and their water was fresh. Once they were settled in, she headed down the aisle until she came to her faithful mare, Jazzy.

Jazzy stuck her head out of the stall toward Joy and snorted in greeting.

"How are you?" Rubbing Jazzy's muzzle, she giggled when the horse butted her with her massive head. "How about me and you go for a quick ride?"

Jazzy backed away and pranced as if to answer.

"I thought you'd say that," Joy murmured.

She needed something else to occupy her mind. Riding Jazzy would be just the thing to distract her from Wade Brooks and all his sexiness.

After getting Jazzy prepped, Joy led her mare out of the barn. Jazzy let out a snort and glanced at Joy.

"Hell yeah, I'm ready," Joy snickered. Hefting herself up into the saddle, she grabbed the reins and turned Jazzy in the direction she wanted. The horse trotted along until they arrived behind the barn. "Yaw!"

Jazzy took off.

Her hooves dug into the ground and ate up the distance. Jazzy must have been a mind reader, sensing Joy desired the wind in her hair, and to feel the power of her magnificent beast underneath her.

Joy grinned as they tore up the dirt path, one they had traveled many times. They rounded the bend and came out into a beautiful area. Jazzy slowed to a trot.

"Whoa," Joy commanded.

Jazzy followed Joy's orders and halted. Dismounting, she took the reins in her hand and walked with her mare alongside her.

"It is such a beautiful day."

Jazzy snorted, as if to agree. Joy glanced at her and laughed. If someone caught her talking to her horse, they would lock her up for sure.

They came to a section where Joy loved to sit and gaze upon her family's land near a large oak tree. She released Jazzy to allow her to graze while she took a seat by the tree's base.

Breathing in deep, Joy relaxed and kicked off her shoes. It was one of her favorite spots to come when she wanted to get away from everyone.

She dug her feet in the grass and stared off at the land her family had worked for years. There would be no thoughts of chores, work, or sexy cowboys named Wade Brooks.

3

"Have you been practicing?" Wade laughed, watching Tyler trot around the corral on his horse, Rocky.

Tyler beamed as he guided Rocky over to Wade.

Wade rested his forearms on the fence, pride filling him with how well his nephew was taking to the ranch. Tyler loved living there, and had flourished. When Wade had first met the kid, he was unaware they were related, but something at the back of his mind told him the kid was familiar to him. At that moment, he couldn't put his finger on it, but when Wade saw Tyler and Parker in the same room, it clicked.

Tyler was a smaller version of Wade's older brother.

The kid had wiggled his way into Wade and Carson's hearts. He was one of the fellas, and hung out as much as he could with his uncles and Father.

He was pure Brooks. He had a love for the land, the horses, and the open sky.

If only their father had been so accepting of Tyler's mother ten years ago, their lives would have been so different.

Wade knew his father could be one mean son of a bitch, but the manipulation the old man went through so that Parker wouldn't end up with Maddy was a new low.

When the shit hit the fan, and Parker had confronted their father about his involvement in Maddy leaving, Jonah's heart couldn't stand it.

The old man fell down and had a heart attack. He came close to dying, but Heaven, nor Hell, was ready for the ornery rancher, and sent him back.

After an extended hospital stay, he was discharged to a rehab facility to get stronger. Wade and his brothers arranged for a nurse to come stay with Jonah so they could concentrate on the ranch.

It was the best idea any of them could have come up with.

Now that Jonah was back at home, things on the ranch were tense. Maddy and Jonah hadn't spoken one word to each other that Wade was aware of, and he didn't blame her.

One look at Tyler, it was obvious he was a Brooks. No blood test was warranted. Jonah had no choice but to accept his grandson. The one thing the elder Brooks stood by was their family.

A Brooks man always took care of his family.

"I've been working with Rashad after my chores," Tyler announced. He sat atop his horse as if he'd been doing it his entire life. Rocky and the kid had hit it off from the moment Parker introduced them. Parker had done a great job of picking out a horse for his son. Rocky was calm and patient with Tyler.

"I can tell. You're doing great. With your non-dominant hand, you want to keep the rope to have a little more slack." Wade demonstrated the technique. He and his brothers had been roping calves since they were Tyler's age. "You'll swing your arm like this, so that way, you'll be able to control it before it leaves your hand."

Tyler paid close attention to Wade's instructions. He was a quick learner. He had Parker's love for the land, but he definitely had Maddy's smarts.

"Got it." Tyler turned Rocky and took off around the perimeter of the fence. His form was close to impeccable as he swirled the rope, making perfect circles in the air. The young cattle, scared, took off, scrambling to get away. Tyler's focus was narrowed in on the cow. His aim was accurate, and the top landed around the small cow's neck.

"Attaboy!" Wade clapped, cheering on his nephew. Pride filled him. Spending time with Tyler had Wade thinking that maybe his father was right about one thing.

It was time for him to settle down.

But like Parker, he would rather do it his way.

Their father always went on about how they needed to find daughters of prominent families, but that wasn't how he wanted to go about it.

Wade wanted to find that special woman to spend the rest of his life with. Not a business merger between ranches.

He wanted someone who was beautiful, intelligent, sexy, and understood the ranching life. It wasn't glamorous, but hard work. Any woman who captured his attention would need to be a spitfire and be able to handle whatever he threw at her.

Not someone who would only be interested in his wealth.

A connection was necessary.

An image of a sassy sheep rancher came to mind, and Wade paused. That woman had a mouth on her, and whenever Wade was around her, he didn't know if he wanted to put her over his knee or kiss her.

His phone chirped from his back pocket. He pulled it out, seeing a message from Maddy.

Send Tyler home, please.

Wade shook his head. "Tyler, your mom said it's time for you to come home."

"Aw, come on." The kid's shoulders slumped. He glanced over at Wade with a pleading look. "Can you ask her for more time?"

"You're not getting me in trouble." Wade laughed as he motioned Tyler toward the barn. "These calves ain't going nowhere. You take Rocky back to the barn and get him brushed down, watered, and fed."

"Yes, Uncle Wade." The kid's lip practically dragged on the ground. He dismounted from Rocky and grabbed the reins. "Let's go, Rocky."

Wade sent off a quick text that he'd delivered the message and was having Tyler put Rocky up.

He slid his phone back in his pocket and hopped over the fence so he could get the calves back to their mommas. Once the calves had been moved, Wade headed toward his truck.

He wanted to check in on his father and the new nurse, Eliana.

Since Jonah had arrived back at the ranch, they had gone through four nurses. The poor women couldn't handle the gruff, ornery old man.

Eliana was the fifth, and so far, she was the only one who had lasted. She was a pretty, yet older woman who wouldn't take any crap from the sixty-year-old rancher.

She came to the ranch about five times a week to

check up on Pops. She ensured his medications were right, and even cooked for him.

That was probably what snagged Jonah.

Jonah was a Brooks, and they all had a weakness for pretty women who could cook. Wade's mother had been a fantastic one.

God rest her soul.

Grace Brooks had been one strong woman to put up with Jonah. She'd raised three boys while being the wife of a rancher. She'd passed away from lung cancer when Wade was in the eleventh grade.

Ain't life a bitch.

She'd never picked up a single cigarette in her life, but that was what took her from this world.

Once inside his truck, Wade guided it toward the main house. He drove along the winding road that led to the house he was raised in. It was mid-summer, and it was a beautiful day to roll with the windows down. The wind blew into the truck, and it felt good.

The Blazing Eagle was one of the largest ranches in the county. They had more head of cattle than anyone around. Wade was proud of their homestead. They owned thirteen thousand acres and were all able to have their own houses on the property.

The love for Blazing Eagle was something Wade couldn't explain. Gazing out on the rolling hills, bright-green grass, and bright-blue sky calmed him.

This was home.

None of the Brooks' siblings could tolerate living with their father. When they'd gotten the chance, they'd built their own homes on the family land. Wade and his brothers had beautiful, sprawling homes, and were only a few minutes' drive from each other.

As long as Wade had breath in his body, he'd live on this land. It was purchased by his great-great-great-grandfather, and had been passed down through the generations. When his father decided to turn over full operations of the ranch, Wade and his brothers would be splitting ownership evenly.

Wade arrived at the main house and parked. Eliana's car was in front of the garage.

Wade got out of his truck and headed toward the stairs.

"Hey, Pop. How's it going?" Wade asked.

Jonah had lost some weight. He had always been a tall, stocky man. When Wade was a kid, his father appeared larger than life. Now, after an extended hospitalization and rehab stay, he was a shell of his former self. Hopefully, now that he was home, he'd put back on the weight he'd lost. Eliana's cooking is amazing, and she made sure Jonah always ate.

A physical therapist came out to the house a couple times a week to work with Jonah on strength building.

Between therapy and Eliana's food, Wade was sure Jonah would be back to his usual self soon.

"Bored out of my damn mind," Jonah grunted. He sat in the rocking chair, staring out onto the property. "I'm ready to get back up on my horse."

"Not sure if it's time yet." Wade bit back a chuckle and leaned against the pillar. He shook his head and knew he would feel the same.

"It's been too long. A man needs to feel his faithful steed underneath him and travel the land he owns." Jonah sat still, his gaze shifting toward the yard.

"We've been taking care of everything."

Jonah looked at him and snorted. "That's not what I said. I'm sure you boys are taking care of the ranch, but I need to see it for myself. My blood, sweat, and tears are on this ranch, and I need to see it, walk it, and breathe it in. This is my life."

The door opened, and Eliana walked out onto the porch. She took a seat next to his father, who glanced at her before returning his gaze to their surroundings.

Wade didn't miss the way his father's eyes softened slightly when he took in Eliana's smile.

He held back a smirk.

His father was smitten.

"What are you out here complaining about, Jonah?" she asked.

"I'm going out on my horse today. Y'all can't stop me," Jonah replied gruffly.

"Are not. You're not ready yet," Eliana quipped.

"I can take you out in one of the four wheelers. We'll drive out as far as you want," Wade offered. It would do the old man some good to feel the wind in his face and breathe in the fresh air. Wade could understand his father's request. He also loved just looking out at what his ancestors had built from the ground up.

"That's not the same," Jonah snapped. He turned his gray eyes on Wade and glared at him.

When Wade was a kid, that one look would have him scrambling to do whatever his father commanded. Now, it did little for Wade. He was a grown man who could handle what his father threw at him. He had inherited Jonah's stubbornness, and didn't back down from him.

Wade was prepared to go to war with his father.

Jonah Brooks would not be getting on his horse today.

"Four wheeler or nothing," Wade sniffed, and slid his hands into his pockets. He could do this all day. It didn't bother him.

"Jonah Brooks!" Eliana turned in her chair and faced him. "You are better off doing what Wade is suggesting. What if you fall off the horse? You aren't as young as you used to be, and I'm not taking care of you with broken bones."

Jonah looked as if he was going to put up a fuss, but the moment he met Eliana's gaze, he did the unthinkable.

"Okay, Wade. We'll do it your way," his father responded.

Wade almost slid off the pillar in shock.

Did Jonah just agree he was right?

Hell had officially frozen over.

There had only been one other woman who could get Jonah Brooks to do what she wanted, and she was buried out in the family plot.

Was Jonah smitten with Eliana? What was going on here between the two?

Wade grinned. He didn't care. She was the best thing for his father right now, and he vowed he was going to do whatever he must to keep her around.

"Give me a few minutes, and I'll be right back." Wade pushed off and ran down the stairs. He couldn't wait to share this new information with his brothers.

Eliana took no shit from Jonah. Maybe that was what Jonah had been missing since his wife had died.

The attention of a good woman.

Hell, didn't they all?

The wind blew through Wade's hair as he drove the small vehicle along the dirt road. His father sat next to him, appearing content at gazing out onto the land they owned.

It had been a while since Wade had spent quality time alone with his father. It was quite difficult since he had been in the hospital, and then his short stint in rehab.

Jonah Brooks was a difficult man, one who took some getting used to being around.

Well, Wade had spent his entire life on this ranch, and his father, he could deal with.

He pulled up to the edge of the road where it died off and became nothing but grass.

"Here fine?" Wade asked.

"Yeah," Jonah muttered, already getting out of the roadster.

Wade killed the engine and took the key out. He hopped out and walked around to where his father stood. "Beautiful day we're having."

"That, it is." His father balanced with his cane and took a few steps into the grass.

"Wait up, Pop." Wade joined him to walk alongside him. No matter what Jonah thought, he wasn't as strong as he used to be. It was going to be a long road to recovery for him.

If anyone searched the word stubborn, Jonah

Brooks' photograph would appear. That was the one thing each of the sons inherited from him.

"I'm no baby. I can walk," Jonah snapped. His eyes cut to Wade and narrowed on him.

Wade didn't offer him a hand or arm, because his father was bullheaded.

"Y'all treat me like I'm a newborn calf. It was my heart that went out, not my legs or brain."

"If we don't look out for you, then who will?" Wade challenged him. "You were so damn mean to the nursing staff, I'm sure you wouldn't be accepted back."

"Didn't need to be in no stinking nursing home anyway," Jonah huffed.

They came upon a stump from a tree that had been struck by lightning. They'd cut it down last summer and used it for firewood.

Wade noted the way his father's breathing pattern had changed. It was slightly labored, and there were tremors in his hands. Wade guided Jonah over to the stump and motioned for him to take a seat.

For once, Jonah didn't argue. He plopped down and sighed.

"Carson worked on that new tractor I purchased from the auction. It's running like it's brand new," Wade announced. He walked a few steps from Jonah and saw how high the grass was growing in the area. They would need to have one of the hands cut it.

"You boys are good sons," Jonah said.

Wade slowly turned around and eyed his father. He wasn't sure where he was going with this. Jonah Brooks never praised his sons for anything.

At the moment, his father appeared every one of his sixty years.

"If someone were to ask me about the one thing I was proud of in my life, I would say my boys." Jonah's gaze was locked on the rolling land before them. "All the money and land doesn't compare to the feeling a father gets when he sees how his boys grew up to be good men."

"You have much more time ahead of you, Pop." Wade walked toward his father. Worry filled him. He was speaking as if he wasn't going to be around too much longer. "You're doing your therapy, and Eliana is making sure you take your pills. By the looks of it, fattening you up too."

Jonah smirked, and it was the closest thing to a smile Wade had seen on the old man's lips in a while.

"That woman doesn't take no for an answer. She just keeps cooking and baking," Jonah grunted. "She acts as if she's trying to feed an army."

"She seems to be sweet on you too." Wade crossed his arms and stared at his father.

"You need to get your eyes checked, boy." Jonah glanced at him and shook his head.

"Let her spoil you. It's been a while since you've had the attention of a woman." Wade grinned. He was sure Jonah still had that old Brooks charm. Their mother had seen something in him and fell in love, married him, and gave him three boys.

His father waved his hand at him. "You boys don't know anything. I haven't been *alone* all these years, ya know."

Wade's eyebrows rose high.

"I've had a lady friend here and there. It took me a while, but loneliness won, and I..." He sighed.

This was a side of Wade's father he was unfamiliar with. There were many sides to Jonah Brooks, and vulnerability had never been one of them.

"Are you telling me that you've—"

"That's none of your business, boy." The twinkle in his eyes had Wade taking a step back and holding his hands up.

Well, damn. Jonah still had it.

"Good for you, Pop," Wade said. He strode forward and rested a hand on Jonah's shoulder. "No more talk as if you aren't going to be here. There's a new generation walking this land, and you're needed."

Jonah nodded.

There was no need for Wade to make it any clearer. Jonah had wanted his boys to ensure their legacy was secured. Parker was starting on his line;

Tyler was the future. He was the first of many grandkids Wade was sure were to come for the patriarch of the Brooks family.

One day, the ranch would be full of young Brooks running around, just like Wade and his brothers had.

"Is it true?" Jonah asked.

"What?" Wade released him. He moved over to the other side of the stump and took a seat next to Jonah. Wade was not in any rush to do anything else today. The last time he'd spoken this much with his father was when Jonah was laid up in the hospital, unconscious. The doctors and nurses had encouraged them to talk out loud or read to their father to help him. Wade wasn't sure if it worked, or if Jonah had heard him, but Wade just sat in the hospital room next to Jonah's bed and talked.

"Parker and Maddy are expecting again?"

The tension between Parker and Jonah was still there. Conversation between the two was usually focused only on the ranch and business dealings. His older brother was very protective of his woman and child.

"Yeah, Pops." Wade leaned forward and rested his forearms on his knees. "We need you to make everything right with Parker and Maddy. Those grandkids are going to need you around to help teach them, just like you taught us."

"There is plenty for everyone." Joy laughed, throwing more of the feed onto the ground. The sun had just graced the sky with its presence, the warm rays comforting and peaceful. Though, the chickens milling around her were impatient this morning. Usually, her mother fed them, but she wasn't feeling well today.

A summer cold was beating her mother down. One look at her, and Joy had tucked her back into bed with the promise that she'd take care of things. Georgina, or Georgy, Whitaker, wasn't a woman who slacked at her work. Georgy had helped run the ranch from the second she'd married Joy's father, Davis.

But today, she relented and got back into bed.

Joy wanted to finish her mother's chores so she could go and help her father. He was currently using the dogs to move the livestock.

The Whitakers were hard-working sheep farmers who raised and bred domestic sheep, providing meat, milk, and wool. It was an intense, but rewarding life career. Joy was proud of her family's business. They had done it for generations, and she was sure their farm would be around for much longer.

The sounds of the dogs barking in the distance grabbed her attention. It was different than their usual tone when herding the sheep.

"What is going on?" She quickly finished tossing the feed to the impatient hens. She even had to step over a few of them as they dove around her for it. "Y'all are acting as if you haven't been fed in a day." The chickens were all fat and well-nourished. They were just being greedy.

She walked over to the inside of the small shed where they kept the supplies for the chicks and hens to put the bucket up. She left and went in search of the dogs. It didn't sound as if they were with her father anymore.

One thing to know about raising sheep was that they were highly intelligent, and could even be taught to follow commands. A few orders, and the entire flock would obey Joy.

The dogs were now in complete guard mode. Joy hurried on, following their yips and warnings. She finally came upon them on the other side of the large barn where they housed their machinery.

She stopped and blew out a deep breath. The dogs

had found a few rogue cows who had broken through the fence that separated Whitaker and the Brookses land.

Lacy, Minnie, and Duke were barking their hearts out, trying to scare the stubborn cows who weren't paying them any attention.

The cattle just grazed as if the three dogs weren't even there.

Damn Brooks and their cows.

They always broke through the fences and caused trouble for her. There was no reason for her to even check to see who owned them.

She knew.

Pulling her phone from her pocket, she searched for Wade Brooks. She could have chosen to call either of the brothers, but her heart did a little pitter-patter when she thought of him. His name appeared, and her breath caught in her throat as she hit the button and waited.

She rolled her eyes while listening to it ring.

"Hello?" he answered on the second ring. His deep, baritone voice sent a tremor down her spine.

"Brooks, your cows are on my land," she stated matter-of-factly.

The cows ambled around without a care in the world, while the dogs were trying their best to push them back to where they'd come from. She took the phone away from her ear and sent a shrill whistle for the dogs. They instantly quit their yapping and came to her side.

"Down," she commanded.

They took to the ground and sat at her feet, but their focus was still on the cows. They would obey her, but they were dying to get back to the cattle. They were good herding dogs, but they were also protective of the area. There were plenty of times they had chased off foxes and coyotes attempting to snatch a small lamb or chicken. They worked well as a team to protect the animals and the property.

"Why do you have my cows?" he drawled when she got back on the line.

Red clouded her vision.

"I didn't take your stinking cows. They broke through your cheap fences and are working my dogs to death," she bit out through clenched teeth. How dare he insinuate she'd taken his animals.

The dogs slowly sat up on their hind legs, itching to run back over to the cows. They growled low as they watched the cattle continue to stroll around and eat.

"I'm coming," Wade announced in his usual calm manner. "Give me fifteen minutes, and don't let any harm come to them."

"They better not harm my dogs—" She paused. The line had gone dead. "Did Wade hang up on me?

How dare he," she huffed. She couldn't wait for him to arrive.

Those damn Brooks brothers had no respect for anyone whose last name wasn't Brooks.

"Go!" She pointed toward the cattle. Maybe she and the dogs could get them back on his land. The dogs took off, barking and working together to try to round them up.

One of the heifers walked away from the dogs and dropped a huge, steamy pile.

"Oh, hell naw! Who is going to clean up this shit?" She stood with her hands on her hips, seething.

Nothing she or the dogs did could get them to move back to their own property. They were just as stubborn as the Brooks men.

Giving up, she called the dogs back and had them go to the barn. The cows seemed as if they weren't going to go anywhere else at the moment. There was nothing around that would harm them.

They were just content where they were.

Joy glanced around, and decided to take a seat under a tree where there was some shade and wait for Wade to arrive. She pulled out her phone and brought up a game to play. There were a million other things she could be doing right now instead of waiting on Wade Brooks to arrive.

She sat in the warm air, actually enjoying these

few minutes of contentment while aligning the colorful balls to get a high score. Her body relaxed back as she continued to play the mindless game. She let out a squeal of excitement, having topped her last score.

Joy looked up for a second to make sure the cattle had not wandered too far off before turning her attention back to her phone.

An engine roared off in the distance. Joy tore her attention away from her silly game to see an ATV pull up on the other side of the fence.

Wade shut off the engine and got out. He'd dressed in tight Levi's, a button-down plaid shirt, and boots.

He was too damn sexy for his own good. Joy scowled at the thought of him being sexy. Why couldn't she push that thought aside? It would be helpful if God made him bald, missing teeth, and with a potbelly. It would be much easier to deal with him without holding back drool whenever she was around him.

He walked through the broken fence, and it was then she realized why she couldn't shake the idea.

Because it was the truth.

He shoved a hand through his hair, and she cursed. He was perfect. If there were a poster board for a hot rancher, Wade Brooks' picture would be there.

There was no doubt about it. Wade was hot as sin.

The epitome of sexy cowboy, and she was taking notice of all his swagger and appeal.

Wade strolled toward her with that irritating grin of his.

"Howdy, neighbor," he greeted.

Joy narrowed her gaze on him. "Is that all you can say, Brooks? And who the hell is going to clean up the cow dung over there?"

She pointed to the area where the cow had left its gift. Wade turned in the direction and let out a low whistle.

"Don't worry about it. We'll get it all cleared up."

"See that you do." Joy stood and put her phone in her back pocket before folding her arms.

His eyes scanned her from head to toe. She tried not to fidget in place to show it bothered her, but deep inside, she wanted to know what he thought of her. It was always so hard to read him, but most of the time, he was too busy pissing her off.

"How about for all the trouble, I take you out to dinner?"

She froze in place, unsure if she had heard him correctly. Did he just say he would take her out to dinner? There had to be a catch. She glanced around, but didn't see anyone else. So this wasn't a joke? She half expected to find someone watching them.

"Why? What else did you do?" she asked.

Curiosity filled her. Had he hit his head before he arrived?

He barked out a laugh and came over to stand closer to her. She had to tilt her head back to meet his gaze. He was a big guy, and she always felt dainty when standing beside him.

"Nothing, Joy. I just wanted to make up for the trouble. I'll have some of the hands come fix the fence and clean up the mess. You won't even be able to tell the cows had made their way onto your property."

Joy brushed her hands on her jeans. "That's all I want. No need for dinner."

Her heart pounded at the thought of being alone with him—those gray eyes of his bore into hers as he took her in.

Dammit, her body was betraying her. Whenever she was around Wade, and he looked at her with those stormy eyes, she instantly became aroused. It had been a long while since she'd been touched by the opposite sex.

Not that she couldn't have a man. It was just that the last relationship she had been in ended amicably. Since then, she'd poured all her focus into the ranch. Now that she thought about it, she and Jason had broken up two years ago.

"I know I pissed you off the other day at the auction. Let me make it up to you."

Joy had to hand it to him. He was certainly one stubborn man. She chewed on her lip, trying to decide on what to do.

"What makes you think you pissed me off?" She raised her eyebrows. She hadn't thought he'd noticed she was pissed. He had been a grouch at the auction, and it wasn't until they'd met again at the gas station that he'd acted like a gentleman.

He shrugged. "I said some things, you said some things. We could smooth everything out between us over a good meal. After all, we are neighbors, and we should be cordial with one another."

She gnawed on her bottom lip and thought for a second.

"When?" she asked.

He moved closer, and his scent floated through the air. She breathed it in, and her walls weakened.

Jesus. What cologne did he wear? It was like an aphrodisiac. Her body swayed toward him, needing to breathe more of it in.

"Tonight," his deep voice replied. "It will be just the two of us—as neighbors."

A strand of his hair fell forward into his eyes. He brushed it back, and her heart did that little dance it did when she was around him. She found herself nodding.

"Great. I'll pick you up at seven." His grin spread across his face.

What the hell did she just agree to?

Joy stormed into her room in a panic. What did one wear when going out to dinner with their neighbor?

Throwing open her closet door, she concentrated on her clothing. What would be appropriate?

Jeans?

Hell, no. Joy always wore jeans.

A skirt?

Maybe. She riffled around until her hand landed on a dress she'd purchased on a whim and had yet to wear. She wasn't sure where they were going for dinner, but it would be perfect.

It was an off-the-shoulder dress that flowed around her knees. It was white with large flowers on it, and had made her feel feminine.

Grinning, she pulled it out and laid it on her bed. She rushed over to her dresser and found the perfect lingerie. It was black, lace, and one of her favorite sets.

Not that she was planning on him seeing what was underneath her dress.

She always wanted to be prepared.

Just in case.

There was no way she was wearing cotton anything while out with a man like Wade Brooks.

Now, it was time for a shower. She had just come in from working the ranch, and she was pretty sure the scent of sheep shit was embedded in her pores.

Stripping off her clothes, she tossed them into the hamper in her closet before grabbing a towel to wrap around herself.

Exiting the room, she was met by her mother, who was coming out of her bedroom. Georgy was a beautiful woman with short, dark hair and silky brown skin. She didn't look a day over fifty.

"Hey, Ma." She smiled. Joy noticed her mother was dressed in a soft pink blouse, jeans, and sandals. Just where was she off to? "Are you feeling better?"

"I am. I can't remember the last time I laid around in bed for so long. Maybe that was all I needed."

"You do work too hard, Mom." Joy tightened her towel. "I've been telling you for years that you and Dad need to go on a long vacation. Junior and I can handle this place."

"Maybe. Why don't you help me find something, and then I'll try to talk your father into it." Georgy smiled and leaned against the wall. "And what are you up to?"

"About to jump in the shower. I need to feel like a human again."

"Got any plans tonight?" her mother asked.

Joy hesitated. Admitting she was going out to dinner with a Brooks wouldn't go over well.

"Just out with a friend I went to high school with." That was a safe answer. It wasn't lying, since she and Wade were the same age and graduated from high school together.

"Sounds fun." Georgy pushed off and rubbed Joy's shoulder. "Your father and I are going to run out for a bit. We shouldn't be gone long."

Joy made her way down the hall and entered the bathroom. She shut the door and blew out a deep breath. Georgy Whitaker was as nosy as they came.

Joy put her hair in a bun so she could cover it before she got into the shower. She walked over to the stall and turned the water on so it could warm up.

She didn't have much time before Wade was due to show up. Dropping the towel onto the floor, she put on her shower cap and stepped under the spray.

"It's just dinner," she muttered, turning around to let the water pound against her back.

Wade's gray eyes, his killer smile, and intoxicating scent came to mind.

Who was she kidding?

If Wade made a move toward her, she would not be coming home tonight.

5

Wade didn't know what made him invite Joy out for dinner, but he'd found himself doing it. His breath had been snatched away when he got closer to her. She had been shooting daggers at him with her eyes as soon as he had stepped foot onto her property.

The cattle breaking out and going onto her land was a problem.

In the back of his mind, he knew he needed to smooth things over with her, and dinner was the first thing that popped into his mind.

It was obvious she was contemplating his offer. The moment she'd bitten her lower hip, his cock had taken notice.

The sun's rays had shined on her beautiful bronze skin perfectly. Her beauty called to him, and that spitfire attitude of hers kept him on his toes.

He would have to admit that Joy Whitaker had captured his attention. He wasn't sure why she was still single, but it worked to Wade's advantage. She used to date one of the guys who had worked on another ranch, but he didn't remember hearing what had happened between them.

Wade took one last look at himself in the mirror and cringed. He was overdue for a haircut, and vowed to make an appointment soon. It was getting too long, and kept falling in his eyes.

"Nothing I can do about it now," he muttered. He flipped the light out in his bathroom and walked through his master bedroom. He snatched his keys, wallet, and phone off the nightstand by his bed. Slipping his wallet into his pocket, he left his room.

Wade had built this house about five years ago from the ground up, as living with his father was no longer an option. He'd worked with the builder to construct the beautiful house.

It was larger than one man needed on his own. One day, Wade hoped to fill it with a family.

He couldn't wait.

Parker was the first of them to take the plunge, and would be getting married soon. He and Maddy already had Tyler, and would soon be adding to their small family.

Wade was slightly jealous of his older brother, but was happy for him. Maddy and Tyler were ideal for Parker.

Arriving at his front door, Wade pulled it open and found Carson coming up the stairs of the porch.

"Where you going dressed all fancy?" Carson teased.

Wade rolled his eyes and stepped out onto the porch, shutting the door closed behind him.

"None of your business." He slid his phone in his front shirt pocket and eyed his brother.

"Oh, secrets. You smelling all good, it's got to be with a woman." Carson laughed. He put up his fist and pretended to jab at Wade.

"What do you want?" Wade chortled, blocking his brother's blows.

"Well, I came to see if you wanted to go out for a beer or something." Carson moved back and twisted his baseball cap around.

"Not tonight. Got plans." Wade jogged down the stairs with Carson following behind him. "Maybe some other night."

"Yeah. I'll call Kyson and see what's he's up to." Carson slapped him on his shoulder, then headed toward his truck. "Well, if it is a woman, then here's hoping you get lucky tonight."

"Ass," Wade muttered.

His younger brother was always a jokester. Wade shook his head and got into his pickup. If he would have shared where he was going and with whom,

Carson would never have left. Carson blew his horn before driving off.

Wade wasn't sure why he was nervous. He started the engine and eased out. He drove down the gravel road that led to the main street.

The sound of her slight country twang on the phone was downright sexy. He loved getting a rise out of her. He loved when she was pissed at him. Hell, she was always pissed at him for something whenever they spoke or were in the same place.

He grinned, thinking of what she'd looked like when he'd shown up. If it were possible, smoke would have been streaming from her ears.

Thoughts of what she would look like under him, over him, in front of him, had plagued his mind for days.

He ran a hand along his face.

Joy Whitaker, naked and spread out on his bed, was one image he couldn't shake. What he wouldn't do to be able to make that fantasy a reality.

"Shit," he groaned. He had to push those fantasies from his mind. If he showed up with a raging hard-on, she'd probably go off on him about that.

Not that he would blame her.

Tonight was supposed to be two neighbors going out for dinner. Their fathers may not get along, but that didn't mean they couldn't.

Wade rolled the window down to let some air in, needing to cool down. Within minutes, he was turning onto the road that led to the Whitaker's home. Their property wasn't as large as the Brookses spread. Sheep farmers didn't need as much land as cattle ranchers. Sheep didn't consume as much, and were content on smaller fields.

The Whitaker home came into view. It was a beautiful country house with a wraparound porch. The woodwork was impeccable. The home had wooden pillars that were bold and natural, while the rest of the house was painted white. It gave off a feel of old-world country with new modern fixtures.

Wade parked the truck on the edge of the driveway, next to the walkway up to the house. He killed the engine, and had to bat down the butterflies that appeared in his stomach. He stepped out of the vehicle, unsure of what to expect. If Davis Senior came to the door, he'd probably have his shotgun in hand.

Walking up the pathway, he arrived at the base of the stairs when the door opened. He froze, speechless.

Joy was in a dress that stopped just above her knees, and her shoulders bare. Sandals displayed her dainty toenails painted hot pink. She had a small purse hanging from her shoulder.

She scowled. "What's wrong?"

He shook his head. "Nothing. Never seen you in a dress before."

"So, you think I run around in jeans and sheep dung all day?" she huffed

The fire in her eyes had him grinning. He'd bet she was a hellcat in the sack. He swallowed hard. There he went again. He had to push all images of sex and Joy Whitaker to the back of his mind.

He was a gentleman, and his mother, God rest her soul, would probably haunt him if he said what he was truly thinking.

"Maybe jeans, but not shit," he replied.

Her hands went to her hips. He walked up the stairs and stopped right in front of her. She tipped her head back, allowing her dark hair to flow over her bare shoulders. Her big brown eyes were done in makeup, highlighting how pretty they were. He itched to touch her, but she might kick him in the balls if he laid a hand on her.

"You smell too good right now. If that's what sheep dung smells like, then I'm in the wrong business."

She relaxed slightly, giving a hesitant smile. He was winning her over. It wouldn't be fun if they were arguing all night.

"Where are we going?" she asked.

"I figured we go to Pin Pushers." Pin Pushers was a popular bar and bowling alley in town. The food was out of this world, the alcohol was good, and the atmosphere was always upbeat and fun.

A glint appeared in Joy's eyes, and Wade groaned. He knew that look. She was up to something.

"I'll be right back." She turned and ran back into the house, slamming the door shut behind her.

He leaned against the pillar and waited patiently. The sounds of Joy's dogs yapping in the house could be heard in the quiet.

What the hell was she doing?

A few seconds later, she came out of the house with a bowling bag. "Now I'm ready."

"What is that for?" he scoffed, following her down the stairs.

"If I'm going to whip your ass at bowling, then I need to make sure I do it properly," she snickered.

Only Joy couldn't put aside her competitive streak for a night.

"I think it would take more than a special ball to beat me," he teased.

She turned to him with her lips curled up in the corners. He was drawn to this playful side of Joy. He liked seeing her smile. Her features brightened, and he found himself moving closer to her as they walked to the truck.

"Shit talking now, are we?" Her perfectly sculpted eyebrows rose. She used her elbow to nudge him. "I'll have you know, this is more than a special ball, Wade Brooks."

They arrived at the truck. Wade couldn't help it any longer. He rested his hand at the small of her back to guide her to the passenger door. Her body fit beside his quite nicely.

His cock reacted too. He bit back a groan and tried to will it down.

"Really? And what is it?" He gripped the handle and waited for her response.

She giggled. "It is the ball I'm going to beat you with."

He joined her, laughing at her silliness. She looked down at his hand on the door and back up to him, as if shocked.

"What? You seem to think I don't have any manners." This time, it was him who raised his eyebrows at her. He took her bowling bag from her and opened the door.

Joy slid her hand into his waiting one so he could help her up into the cab.

He ignored the electrical current that rushed through his arm when their fingers touched.

"Well, you Brooks men have been known for a few things. Not sure if manners were ever mentioned." She brushed against him as she stepped up onto the running board.

Her soft curves felt divine, and he had a suspicion she had done it on purpose.

Well, if that was the case, two could play that game.

"Guess I'll have to show you what us Brooks men are really known for." He shut the door.

Her shocked face met his through the window. He couldn't help but toss a wink her way.

He walked around to his side and opened the door. He slid her bag onto the back seat then hopped in. Already, her scent filled the cab. It was light and floral, teasing his senses. He wanted to bury his face into the crook of her neck so he could breathe it in.

"So, what exactly are Brooks known for? I want to compare my notes."

Wade grinned and hit the button to start the engine. He glanced over at Joy, who was studying him intently. Her lips were plump, and he wondered what they would taste like.

Drive, man.

Dinner. Bowling.

He had to remind himself what they were in the truck for. He put it in reverse and turned it around in their small circle of a drive and headed back to the main street. It took everything in him not to drive toward his place.

"Not sure if that's something we should be

discussing since we are just two friendly neighbors going out for dinner," he joked.

She playfully pushed him. "Oh, no. You opened Pandora's box, and I want to know. Come on, Brooks, fess up. What are you Brooks men known for?"

He feigned a cough, and kept his focus on the road ahead.

"Let's just say this. Depending on how our night goes, you may figure it out on your own."

"Are you sure you will be able to bowl in that dress?" Wade asked.

Joy looked up from tying her shoes and grinned.

"Is that worry I hear in your voice, Brooks?" she challenged.

If it were, he was a smart man. Joy had loved to bowl since her father first introduced it to her when she was five years old. There was something about taking one's frustration out in throwing a heavy ball at some pins that seemed to satisfy her.

Joy and her family had spent plenty of weekends at the bowling alley. It gave them a break from the constant hustle of sheep farming. She and her friends indulged in games while the adults sat around drinking, talking, and having a good time.

"Never that," he taunted.

He stood from his perch on the bench across from her, and she eyed the way he filled out his jeans and the long-sleeved shirt. He grinned at her while he folded up his sleeves to reveal his forearms.

Joy swallowed hard, and had to beat down the twinge of arousal the simple act elicited.

He knew what he was doing.

There was no way he didn't know the effect he would have on a woman.

He refused to indulge her in the truck and share with her what Brooks men were really known for, but she could guess.

It didn't take a rocket scientist to know the Brooks brothers had a reputation. The buckle bunnies followed them around. Tales of Wade, Parker, and Carson's party antics were shared around town.

They were legendary.

Drinking, partying, fighting, and women.

She'd heard all about the three of them. What was embellished versus real, she didn't know.

When they were in high school, girls threw themselves at them on a daily basis, and Joy was sure that now they were adults it was no different.

The years had been good to Wade. No longer was he the skinny boy she'd grown up hating from afar. Now he was a man who was filled out with hardened muscles from working the land daily.

And she was secretly lusting after him.

She rolled her eyes and gazed at their

surroundings. Pin Pushers had gone through a massive renovation recently. It had been around for decades, and was considered a staple in town. They'd updated the place to be trendy, and it had paid off.

It was packed tonight with plenty of people hanging out. There was bowling, bocce, pool, and a bar. Everything a small town needed to have fun on a weekend. It had a great patio that was popular in the summer as well.

There weren't many places like this in town. For bigger establishments, one would need to go to one of the larger cities for entertainment.

Wade and Joy had their own private section. It was roomy enough for a tiny party, but since it was just the two of them, there was plenty of space for them to spread out.

"Hey, y'all, I'm Sandy. Can I take your order?" A middle-aged woman with dark hair asked, her pad and pen at the ready.

Wade walked over to her and took a seat next to Joy on the leather bench.

"Anything good?" he asked, holding up the menu for both of them to see.

Joy leaned over and leaned against his shoulder so she could read it.

Wade's cologne was a distraction. It floated around

her, wrapping her up in his scent. She had to focus on the words for them to compute.

"Right . The open-face grilled salmon is my favorite." Sandy perked up and went into the description of the sandwich. She mentioned a few other items that were on special. Pin Pushers Bistro had been the talk of the town. The owners had invested in hiring chefs who redid their menu, and it was a success. This was the first time Joy had been inside the building since it reopened.

They put in their orders with Sandy. Of course, Wade being a cattle rancher, ordered a steak dinner, while Joy stuck with the lamb.

No shame in supporting their own industry.

"I'll be right back with your drinks." Sandy snatched up the menu and spun away.

Wade snickered and glanced at Joy.

"What?" she asked.

"Iced tea?"

"What's wrong with that?" She crossed her legs. From past experience, she knew alcohol was like truth serum for her. No way was she having any of her true thoughts of Wade ever coming forth.

"Not a thing." He stood and strolled over to the computer screen, typing out a few commands. "Ladies first."

Joy looked up at the television overhead to see Whitaker versus Brooks on the scorecard. She smirked.

A good old country rivalry was about to commence at the bowling alley.

A party of young women a couple rows away kept throwing appreciative looks toward Wade. An unknown feeling swept over her.

This isn't a date, she chanted, but she couldn't shake the voice in the back of her mind. Wade had surprisingly been the gentleman, opening doors and carrying her heavy bowling bag.

"I hope you're ready for an ass kicking," she joked and stood.

"Those shoes go perfect with that dress," he teased.

She modeled her outfit for him. She gave a twirl, and rested her hands playfully on her hips. Wade smiled, his gaze roaming her body.

Her breath caught in her throat. It was as if she could feel his touch from the heat in his eyes. She sashayed over to him. She didn't know where this flirtatious nature was coming from.

Joy hadn't thought there was a seductive bone in her body.

"I hope you brought you're A game." She ignored the huskiness in her voice and tossed him a wink. Brushing past him, she grabbed her ball and slid her fingers inside the holes.

An older gentleman in the party next to their area was walking up to the line. She paused, waiting patiently for her turn. He strolled forward and tossed his ball, which slid effortlessly down the waxed floor, and slammed into the pins with eight toppling over. His group cheered for him as he went back to them.

Joy narrowed her eyes on her lane and stalked forward. She swung her arm back and threw the ball forward, releasing it. It slid smoothly down the slick wooden floor, crashing into the pins.

Strike!

She fist pumped the air and twirled around, smiling. Wade's eyebrows shot up as he started to clap.

"Impressive."

She threw an extra twitch in her hips as she sauntered back to him. She couldn't help the competitive nature in her. It was in her bones.

She poked him in the chest playfully. "Your turn."

Wade's hand slid down her waist and pulled her to him.

Holy mother of God.

His body was nothing but hard, sculpted muscles. Her knees grew weak, and Joy had to lock them in place to keep them from giving out.

"Watch this," he murmured into her ear. Wade's warm lips brushed ever so slightly against her earlobe. He released her just as fast as he had grabbed her.

She dropped her eyes down to his ass, and the way the jeans highlighted it.

She bit her lip and sighed. Who was she kidding? As much as she wanted to hate Wade, she couldn't. She took a seat and openly watched him. He patiently waited for the woman in the other lane to finish.

He glanced at Joy over his shoulder and winked at her.

Her heart skipped a beat.

"Here you go, hun." Sandy appeared by her, setting their appetizers and drinks down. Wade had ordered a beer, and she'd ordered an iced tea.

"Thank you." Joy smiled and reached for her drink.

Sandy disappeared quickly, rushing off to another party. Joy took a sip of the sweetened tea and turned back to focus on Wade.

Of course, his form was perfect. His ball flew down the lane and slammed into the pins.

Strike!

He spun around, grinning wide.

The competition was on.

Wade was seeing an entirely new side of Joy. He didn't know where it came from but he could feel the pull to be near her. The entire game she was sexy, flirty, and set on teasing him.

The attraction between them was growing.

There was no denying it was there.

The way her hips swayed when she ambled toward the lane drove Wade crazy. The nice shape of her calf muscles, and the little glimpse of her smooth brown thighs, left him strung tight.

His cock had taken notice, and it was a constant battle to keep it down. At the moment, this was one fight Wade was losing.

He'd had a constant hard-on since Joy had walked to him and poked his chest. It was an automatic reaction to tug her to him. The feel of her soft body against his lit a fire in him.

The bowling competition had heated up.

The score was 180 to 178, with Joy in the lead.

In between their turns, they ate their food.

"Here you go, Wade," Sandy announced, placing two shots in front of him. He'd ordered them while Joy was taking her turn.

Joy came back and sat on the leather bench. He wasn't sure why, but he needed her closer.

"Why are you a mile away?" He snagged her hand and pulled her close to him. Joy's body slipped in next to him. He rested his arm on the back of the bench, not caring how it appeared.

This hadn't been a date, but it had all the feels, and he wasn't going to ignore the flirting, sensual looks she had been throwing his way. He was a hot-blooded male, out with a beautiful woman.

Wade was enjoying himself immensely.

"What are these?" Joy asked, pointing to the glass on the table in front of them.

Wade reached for them and handed her one. "Celebrating us burying the hatchet."

She cocked an eyebrow at him. She crossed her legs, and Wade had to fight to keep from looking at the smooth expanse of skin. The fantasy of feeling her supple legs wrapped around his waist was getting harder to resist.

"Are we?" she asked.

Wade blinked, temporarily forgetting what they were speaking about. His gaze met her large brown pools, and he nodded. His tongue was stuck to the roof of mouth. She took the drink from him with a slight smile on her lips.

He raised his glass to hers. "New beginnings."

The light clink of glass filled the air. The background noise faded away, as if it were just the two of them. He was impressed by the way she knocked back the glass. His gaze fell down to the smooth column of her neck. He ached to bury his face into the crook of her neck and breathe in her scent. Her perfume was light, but intoxicating. He did the same, ignoring the slight burn of alcohol. He took their empty glasses and placed them on the table.

Wade leaned back and rested his arm behind Joy. She turned to him, her body fitting snug next to him. She looked up him with a small tilt of her lips.

"This was fun," she admitted.

He nodded again, and his fingers found their way into the dark strands of her hair. Her eyes darkened. He wondered if he leaned in and pressed his lips to hers, whether she would accept the kiss or push him away.

He didn't care if they were in a very public place.

They were both consenting adults.

Her plump lips were calling to him.

Throwing caution to the wind, he dipped his head down and claimed them. He cupped her face as his lips moved over hers. She opened her mouth and welcomed his tongue.

The kiss was short, but packed enough heat to tell him the attraction was not one-sided.

Wade pulled back and opened his eyes. Joy's were slightly out of focus. She blinked a few times before they settled on him. He kept his hand on her face, rubbing her flawless skin with his thumb.

"Wanna go back to your place?" she blurted out.

Wade's heart paused, then began to race in an

erratic manner. She had taken the words right out of his mouth. He inched forward and pressed a soft kiss to her lips.

"Yes, but first,"—Another kiss to her slightly swollen lips—"it's my turn. Don't think you're going to distract me to win."

He grinned wide and stood. He was just as competitive as she was, and wasn't going down without a fight.

Her laughter floated through the air behind him. As rock-hard as his cock was, he wasn't sure he could focus, but dammit, he was going to try his best.

Joy didn't know what came over her. She had never been so bold to ask for a man to take her back to his place. That just wasn't her. And on the first date?

It hadn't started as a date, but as the night progressed, it ended up being a date.

If it walks like a duck and quacks like a duck, then it must be a duck.

Everything about Wade tonight was not what she had assumed. Joy had figured they would have a friendly game of bowling, eat some good food, and then head home.

Boy, had she been wrong.

One heated look from him, the hussy in her came out.

Maybe she could blame it on being single for so long. There was something about a man who wasn't afraid to be a man when out with a woman.

Even though those other women kept eyeing

Wade, not once was his attention drawn to them. They hadn't been shy at all in openly gawking at him. They were well into their cups and had grown louder as the night went on.

He had her feeling as if she were the only woman there.

Wade joked with her, making her smile and laugh more than she had in a long time. The subtle touches, his hands on her waist.

That kiss...holy mother of God.

Her panties had gone up in flames and practically melted off her body. Wade Brooks could have asked her for anything at that moment, and she would have done it.

She had forgotten they were even in the bowling alley.

The second his lips pressed against hers, she'd leaned into the kiss with everything she had. Her body was immediately engulfed in the need to be with him.

"It's my turn. Don't think you're going to distract me to win."

When he'd walked away from her to bowl his turn, Joy knew at that moment she was hooked.

They'd both fought to the bitter end. Wade had ended up beating her by two points. She had gracefully bowed to him.

But, oh, there would be a rematch.

Wade led her from Pin Pushers with their fingers entwined. She held on to his arm and leaned on him.

"I had fun tonight," she remarked.

The parking lot was full of cars, and even thought it was late, some of the people were just arriving.

"Good. I knew you would."

"Hey." She lightly hit in him the stomach.

He feigned as if she had hit him hard.

"What'd you do that for?"

"You Brooks are all arrogant," she muttered.

He squeezed her fingers tight and pulled her in to wrap his arm around her shoulders.

"We have a right to be." He howled when her hand shot out again, slamming into his abs.

She registered the ridges underneath her hand. He barked out a laugh as they reached his vehicle. They walked around to the passenger side with him guiding her back to the door.

"Oh, really? Why is that?"

He moved in closer, closing the gap between them. He reached up and ran a finger down her cheek, cupping her face. She bit back a moan at the feeling of his body and his hardness touching her stomach.

"Well, this Brooks man was out with the hottest woman in town," he murmured. He bent down and brushed his lips against hers.

"I'm listening," she whispered.

Her eyes fluttered closed when he covered her mouth with his. His tongue slipped inside to duel with hers.

He was right. He had a reason to be arrogant.

He could kiss.

Joy was lost in him. She gripped his shirt tight with her fingers as she leaned into him.

It wasn't soft and sensual, but hot and explosive.

The only thing that filled her mind was Wade, and the feeling of his body on hers. She slid her hands up his chest and up his neck to dive into the thick curly hair her fingers were itching to touch.

Joy pulled him closer.

She needed more.

Groaning, Wade tore his lips from hers. Their heavy breathing was the only sound that registered in Joy's mind.

Wade rested his head on hers.

"You still want to go back to my place?" His deep voice vibrated through her.

"Yes," she whimpered.

Wade cursed and kissed her hard before helping her into the truck. Once inside, he leaned in to help put on her seat belt.

Another kiss, and the door slammed shut.

Joy's heart was racing a mile a minute while she

watched Wade stalk around the front of the truck. Her core pulsed with the need to have him inside of her.

The driver's door swung open, and Wade slid into his seat. A few seconds later, and a screeching of tires, they were on the road.

Joy glanced down and took in her hand engulfed by Wade's. Soft country music played while they rode in silence.

Joy sat back and enjoyed the warm breeze blowing in through the open windows. Her hair floated through the air. Tucking her blowing hair behind her ear, she took the time to study Wade as he drove. His focus was on the road, and it gave her an uninterrupted view of his profile.

"Is there something on my face?" he asked.

She smiled. "Nope."

"Then what is it?" He glanced over at her, then turned his attention back to the road.

"Just trying to figure out if there will be boxer briefs, tighty-whities, or nothing."

What. The. Hell?

That one shot of alcohol was to blame.

She was a lightweight.

It had been something on her mind the entire night. With his tight-fitting Levi's, she was betting Wade was a commando type of guy.

Wade chuckled. He brought her hand up to his lips and pressed a kiss to the back of it.

"You're going to have to wait and see."

A small smile lingered on Joy's lips while they continued the drive. Fifteen minutes later, they came upon the turn that led to her family's ranch. Wade shot her another look.

"You're sure?"

Joy nodded. There was no way she was changing her mind. Her body was tense, and beyond aroused. She was strung tight, and she needed Wade to put her out of her misery.

They drove past the road and continued on.

The butterflies in Joy's belly increased.

She thought back to his toast. *New beginnings.*

Tonight, Wade Brooks wasn't the enemy. For too long their families had been against each other.

He again brought her hand to his lips and pressed a kiss to it. Her core clenched. The air in the cab grew thick with sexual tension. She bit her lip and tried to suppress all the fantasies she'd had about Wade.

He guided the truck down the road that led to Blazing Eagle Ranch. They drove under the welcome sign, and she knew she had officially crossed the line of no return.

Minutes later, they arrived on the land that had once belonged to her family. Wade's home was built on it. She pushed down the emotions that swirled around in her chest. She almost felt as if she were betraying her ancestors by stepping foot on it, but what was done in the past had nothing to do with her or Wade.

He parked the truck in front of the attached garage and cut the engine. Silence greeted them. They stared at each other without saying a word.

Wade squeezed her hand before releasing it, then exited the cab.

Joy blew out a deep breath as her heart continued to gallop like a runaway stallion.

There was no turning back now.

Her door opened, and there was Wade, holding out his hand for her. She slid her smaller one into his and allowed him to assist her from the SUV. Wade shut the door and trapped her against it. Her breath caught in her throat when he drew closer. Her hands came up to rest on his hardened chest. She stood on her tiptoes to meet him in a hard, bruising kiss.

He immediately took charge of it, and she allowed him to. His tongue swept into her mouth, commanding the kiss. Her hand rode up his chest, and her fingers entwined at the nape of his neck. She pushed closer to him. A moan escaped her.

Wade's large hand trailed along her torso and down to her ass. He gripped her to him, pressing his hardness to her stomach.

She grew flushed and hot, needing more. Wade released her with a growl.

"Let's go, pretty lady. Let's take this inside," he murmured.

Joy blinked, her chest rising and falling fast. Hell, she wouldn't have complained one minute if he had lifted her up against his truck. He took her hand and tugged her behind him. They walked up on the small porch. She leaned close to him while he dug into his pocket for his keys.

She laughed as Wade fumbled with the key and lock. He finally got the door open and guided her inside.

"Welcome to my home."

Joy moved past him and into the foyer. It was a beautifully decorated. There was a unique light fixture overhead. The first level had an open concept that highlighted a wonderful kitchen. Wade's style could be described as a rustic country, and it was right up Joy's alley.

She turned around and found him leaning against the door, his gray eyes locked on her. They had been one of the first features of his she'd noticed when they had met all those years ago. They were a unique shade of coloring, and one of the things that drew women to the Brooks brothers.

"Do I get a tour?" she asked, waving her hand in the air.

Wade pushed off the door and stalked toward her, stopping within millimeters of her. His heated gaze ripped the air from her lungs.

"Do you really want one?"

"No." She shook her head, her voice barely coming out as a whisper. She was sure there would be plenty of time for her to see his house. Right now, there was only one room she was interested in seeing.

His bedroom.

"Good," he growled. He leaned down and scooped her up, tossing her over his shoulder.

Joy laughed as she wrapped her arms around his waist and held on.

8

"Put me down!" Joy screeched. Her voice echoed through the hallway as Wade stormed toward his bedroom. "You are going to hurt your back."

Wade snorted. He'd lifted bales of hay heavier than her. What did she know?

"Girl, you barely weigh anything," Wade muttered. He arrived at his master bedroom and pushed the door open. There was currently one thing on his mind, and that was getting Joy naked.

All night she had teased him. Those creamy brown thighs were driving him crazy. He had to get his hands, mouth, and tongue on them.

He stalked to the oversized bed and paused next to it. He brought Joy off his shoulder, her body sliding down his. His cock was harder than it had ever been at the feel of her curves brushing against him.

When her dark hair fell across her face, she tucked it away, revealing her beauty.

He liked seeing Joy Whitaker in his bedroom, and vowed this wouldn't be the only time she'd be here.

Wade kept his arm wrapped around her, refusing to let her go. Her breasts crushed between them were divine. He bit back a moan at the feel of her soft curves underneath his hands.

She stared up at him with her large brown eyes, leaning into him. Her hand slid up his chest and played with the top button he'd left undone.

"Here we are," she whispered.

"We are," he responded.

Wade swooped down and captured her lips with his. The taste of the woman in his arms was intoxicating. She gripped his shirt with her hands balled up into tight fists.

His desire for her was rising with each soft moan and whimper that spilled from her lips. Wade's hands went on an exploration mission of their own. He cupped her round, plump ass, and brought her closer to him. He kneaded and squeezed her softness.

His cock surged against his jeans, demanding to be released.

The kiss grew deeper. Wade tilted his head and used his tongue to plunder Joy's mouth. Her hands roamed up and settled at the base of his neck, with her fingers diving into his hair. A shiver flowed down his spine at the sensation of her fingers tugging his strands.

Wade was unable to stop. This woman had seduced him from the moment she had walked out of her house in a dress. All night, he couldn't stop thinking about having those beautiful thighs wrapped around his waist.

Joy's hands slipped down and worked on the buttons. He tore his mouth from hers and yanked his shirt from his jeans. He drew it over his head and tossed it to the floor before kicking off his boots.

"What do you think you'll find?" He cocked an eyebrow. He held back a laugh referencing her comment from the truck.

Grinning, she tapped her chin with her finger. "Nothing."

Her voice was husky, and it was sexy.

"Well, I'm not revealing until you take something off." He cupped her cheek and pressed a hard kiss to her lips. He'd been dying to rip her dress off, but he doubted she would appreciate that.

She walked around him, forcing him to turn around. She rested her hands on his chest and shoved him down in a sitting position on the bed.

His chuckle at her playfulness quickly died once she pulled her dress over her head to show what was hidden beneath the soft material.

Wade's mouth went dry.

Black lace.

Her breasts were enveloped in a nearly see-through strapless bra. He could easily see her areolae. Her waist was tapered, but then flared out. Her panties matched, and were completely sheer.

They didn't hide anything.

Joy pushed her hair from her face and stood in front of Wade with her hands on her hips.

"Like what you see?" she asked, tilting her head to the side.

"Fuck yeah." He cleared his throat, motioning her forward. "Come here, Joy."

She closed the distance between them. Gripping her waist, he looked up at her, a smile playing on her lips.

"I like lingerie."

"I'm glad you do." He smoothed his hands over her skin. The panties didn't cover the entire meat of her ass. He was met with supple skin and released a groan. "This is a pleasant surprise."

"Hey." She giggled, her hands resting on his shoulders. She kneaded them for a moment before cupping his face. "I may be a rancher's daughter and get dirty every day, but this is one way I can still stay in touch with my feminine side."

A teasing glint appeared in her eyes.

He liked it.

The lingerie, he loved it. He secretly vowed to buy her whatever she wanted if she only wore it for him.

He yanked her head to his so he could kiss her. He couldn't help it. Those swollen lips were calling to him. Her lips parted, granting his tongue entrance.

Wade guided her down onto the bed. He rolled them where she was on her back and he was slightly raised over her, settling his lower half into the valley of her thighs. Their lips were still merged together, sliding against each other's in a deep, passionate kiss.

He released her, and pressed hot kisses across jawline and down to her neck. He buried his head into the crook of her neck and breathed in her scent. He nipped her skin, then moved on. His lips made their way to her chest as he glided his hand underneath her back.

As much as he loved the bra, it had to go.

One attempt, and she was freed of the contraption.

He pulled it off and felt like a kid on Christmas morning getting to unwrap his first gift.

Her brown mounds were smooth, and just big enough to fill his hands. Her areolae were brown, and her nipples were beaded into little chocolate buds.

"Jesus," he murmured.

He guided the first one to his lips, taking a taste. Joy's moan shot through him and straight to his dick. He took his time bathing the one breast before switching over to the other. Joy's fingers threaded their way into his hair and held him in place.

The taste of her was mesmerizing. He couldn't get enough of her. He growled and tore himself away from her breasts and continued on his journey to his southern destination. He left a trail of kisses over her belly until he shifted lower on the bed, putting him at eye level with her center.

"Wade," Joy groaned.

He spread her legs wide and took in the small sheer panties covering her. Lowering his head, he placed an open-mouth kiss on her mound. Joy's hips shot off the bed. He chuckled and swept a hand down her thigh, finally getting to touch it. He dropped a kiss on one, teasing Joy.

He knew what she wanted.

There was no need to rush anything.

They had all night.

"What do you want, Joy?" he asked.

He trailed a finger up her panty-covered folds. He could clearly see her through it, and was itching to pull the covering off. But now, it was about building up the suspense. He wanted Joy writhing on the bed, screaming his name until she was hoarse.

"You know what I want," she gasped.

Wade applied more pressure against her folds with his finger. He ran his tongue down her thigh, then nipped the skin with his teeth. She jumped, releasing a squeal.

"No. I want you to say it." He gave her another little love bite and smoothed it out with his tongue. His finger was slowly running up her slit, teasing her. Joy's hips lifted as if seeking relief.

In due time.

"Wade!" she groaned.

He continued dropping kisses on her thighs, moving toward her center, but never going there.

"Tell me what you want," he demanded. His cock was pressing painfully against his jeans, reminding him he would need to discard them soon.

"I need you!" she practically shouted. Her body shifted with her hips thrusting forward against his hand. Her legs were left wide open, exposing herself fully to him.

Wade laughed.

"You can do better than that, Whitaker. Tell me exactly what you want, and I promise to put you out of your misery." He trailed his tongue down her thigh, just where her leg and pelvis met. Her body shook underneath him. "Tell me."

"I swear...dammit, Wade," she whimpered.

Her body shook, but he didn't let up on her with his finger. He pushed down harder, watching her slit part and reveal her pink clit.

"Joy," he growled.

"I need you to lick me," she sobbed.

"Where?" he goaded her.

Her legs flexed shut, then opened again.

He had her.

The second she answered him correctly, he would reward her.

"My pussy," she cried out, her body trembling with need. "Please, Wade. Lick my pussy."

With a growl, he snatched her panties off and threw them over his shoulder. Shoving her legs open wide, he covered her mound with his mouth.

Joy's scream echoed through the room.

One long lick had her crying out his name. Her fingers dove into his hair, pulling on the strands. He had waited patiently for her to reveal to him what she truly wanted.

The taste of Joy exploded on his tongue.

Another lick, and she lost it. Her cries filled the air. Chants, curses, and moans spilled from her lips.

He latched onto her clit, pushing her legs out of the way as they attempted to close on his head.

Joy Whitaker was going to get firsthand knowledge of what Wade Brooks was truly about.

She had pestered him in the truck on what Brooks men were known for.

Tonight, she would discover a talent of his that he was very passionate about.

He introduced a finger deep inside her slick core. Her muscles clenched down around him. He held back a moan. The feeling of her clamping on his dick was going to be magical, but right now, at the moment, it was all about her.

He would get his turn soon.

Wade pulled back his finger, and then a second later, sending it in farther. He flicked her clit with his tongue while he continued to finger fuck her.

"Wade!" she wailed.

The sound of his name of her lips was fucking amazing. He would never tire of it. Her hips thrust forward, setting a rhythm of their own.

He twisted his finger around, and sent it in deep in search of that certain area that would send her to the stars.

Joy's muscles grew taut.

He took his time feasting on her.

Wade was determined to bring the most pleasure she had ever experienced to her tonight.

Her honey slipped from her, and he ensured he lapped it all up. He slid two fingers deep inside her and twisted them around, and her hips lifted off the bed again. Wade latched on to her little bundle of nerves while the trembling of her body increased.

She gripped his hair when she crested.

Joy was a beautiful sight as she rode through the waves of her orgasm.

Her body settled back down on the bed, her chest rising and falling quickly. Her eyes were closed, and there was a small smile on her lips.

Wade withdrew his fingers from her and watched her melt against the pillows. He stood, and flicked open the button of his jeans.

What a beautiful sight she made. A light sheen of sweat covered her body. Her dark hair spread out around her head, as if it were a dark cloud.

He pushed down his jeans and kicked them to the floor.

Joy's eyes flew open. They were slightly out of focus. She blinked, focusing in on him. She grinned.

"Aw, damn. I was wrong."

"Hell no, I'm not walking around commando in jeans." He was a boxer brief man.

Her eyes darkened when her gaze dropped to the large tent his cock was pitching. He eased them down, allowing his cock to spring free. It was erect, and standing at full attention. Joy pushed up on her elbows and unconsciously licked her lips.

A growl slipped from him. He crawled back onto the bed, flipping her over.

"Hey, wait a minute," she chuckled. "I don't get to—"

"Not now." There was no way she could touch him. He was already close to exploding, and that was not an option. He'd never been a minute man before, and wasn't going to start tonight. "I promise, you can do whatever you want later."

He brought her up on her hands and knees. His gaze zeroed in on her ass, and he sighed.

She was made perfectly.

He coasted a hand down her spine and lined up the head of his cock with her opening. He nestled the head through her slick folds.

"You promise?" She glanced over her shoulder at him, and he almost blew his load. The woman was too sexy for her own good.

"Yeah." His voice was strained. He pushed forward slightly inside her warm channel. She was tight, enveloping him in her warm cocoon. He gripped her hips and surged forward until he was buried completely inside of her. "Fuck."

He couldn't help the curse. She was extremely tight, and too damn wet.

He was in trouble.

"Oh, God. Wade." Joy's moan was low and husky. She lowered her head to the pillow while her ass remained up. Her hands gripped the sheets, as if needing something to hold on to. It was the perfect position for Wade to get lost in.

He drew back, and surged forward again.

Wade cried out, unable to stop his hips. They were moving on their own accord. Each thrust sent him farther inside her.

Her pussy welcomed him.

He never wanted to leave.

He was home.

Wade dug his fingers into her hips, holding her steady as his hips quickened their motion. Joy rocked herself back against him.

They moved in sync with each other. Their gasps and cries filled the air. Wade reached out and entwined his fingers in Joy's dark tresses, anchoring her to him.

"Joy," he gasped. He delivered deep, powerful strokes. He tried to think of anything to keep him from releasing so soon.

The cattle.

The conversation with his father.

Hell, mucking up the stables.

Nothing was doing the trick.

Being inside Joy was everything he could have imagined.

He needed her to come again. He wanted to feel the contractions of her pussy around him.

"Play with your clit," he commanded. He wasn't going to last much longer, and wanted her to join him.

"Oh," Joy groaned.

She maneuvered herself to slip her arm beneath her, and soon he could feel the motion of her rubbing herself. Her body trembled.

Fuck.

The familiar tingle in his balls was a warning. They drew up close to his body, and he knew he didn't have long.

"Come on, baby. I need you to come for me again," he muttered. Sweat trickled down the side of his face, but he didn't care.

"Wade. Oh, God, I'm almost there."

"Now, Joy. Come for me now," Wade growled. He shifted his hips and drove deeper inside of her.

She cried out as she crested. Her walls constricted around Wade, and he could no longer hold back. He roared through his orgasm. His hips went into overdrive while he pounded into her, filling her with his release.

A sense of contentment and satisfaction overcame Joy. She opened her eyes and found herself flush against a very naked Wade. His possessive arm was wrapped around her, securing her to him.

Her face was nestled into the crook of his neck. She inhaled the scent of him. His cologne was embedded in her nostrils. She loved the smell of it, and could lie there forever just sniffing him. His warm body was pressed to hers. She bit back a silly smile as the memories of their night together rushed forward.

There wasn't an inch of her body that hadn't been touched by Wade.

His lips, tongue, and hands had been everywhere.

A shiver passed through her at remembering his tongue. It had brought her great pleasure. The memory of it between her legs sent a chill down her spine.

The heat of Wade and the blankets had her feeling relaxed.

She blew out a deep breath and pressed a kiss to his neck. A giggle escaped her from his cock jerking against her leg.

There could be no way he was ready to go again.

Wade's shaft hardened beside her.

Well, I'll be...

Joy pulled her head back and glanced up at him. Wade rested back on the pillow with his eyes closed. His chest rose and fell in a steady rhythm. A shadow of a beard covered his jawline. She trembled at the memory of those prickly hairs brushing the inside of her thighs.

She wasn't ashamed to admit she was now officially addicted to Wade Brooks. Her body tingled from head to toe. He'd been extremely generous in ensuring she was thoroughly satisfied.

Wade shifted in the bed, his other hand disappearing beneath the blanket.

"Morning," his deep voice rumbled in his chest. His hand possessively rested on the swell of her ass.

She stared up into his eyes, and a shyness crept over her. She wasn't sure what to say the morning after. She'd never had a one-night stand before.

"Good morning," she replied.

"I don't know about you, but I'm starving. You hungry?" he asked. He shifted onto his side, pulling his arm from under her. His gaze settled on her while he waited for her to answer.

Joy snagged the blankets and tugged them up, tucking them under her arms. She didn't miss the smirk on his sexy lips.

"Yeah, I'm famished." Her stomach chose that moment to speak up. She covered her face with her hand, mortified.

Wade gently removed her hands from her face. A silly grin played on his lips.

"What are you hiding your face for?" Chuckling, he brought her hand to his lips. "Ain't nothing to be embarrassed about. We burned off some calories last night."

Joy burst out laughing at him. Winking, he threw back the covers and stood from the bed. Her gaze dropped down to his naked form. His body was chiseled in all the right places. There wasn't an ounce of fat on him anywhere. Years of working a ranch was evident. He walked around the bed, a teasing glint in his eyes.

Joy sat up, recognizing his silly side.

She yelped and tried to roll away, but he snatched her from the bed and dragged her out, swinging her up and into his arms.

"Wade!" she cried. Her arms flew around his neck so she could hold on.

"Can't get enough of hearing you scream my name, darling. Before I feed you, we need to shower."

"My hair is going to get wet," Joy cried out, holding on for dear life.

Wade's strong arms held her tight to him. He stepped into the bathroom and turned his confused gaze to her.

"What's wrong with that? It's water," he stated matter-of-factly. The room was very spacious, and tastefully decorated. There was a separate soaking tub, and a double vanity with a walk-in shower. The toilet was hidden away in its own little room.

Joy was in love with the space.

"You wouldn't understand about a woman's hair." She buried her face into his shoulder.

He stopped outside the shower and put her down.

She stood before him, his arm still around her while he reached into the stall. It had twin shower-heads on opposite walls. The sound of the water spray filled the air. Wade focused his attention back on her.

"What's there to understand? Is your hair going to fall off if it gets wet?"

"No." Joy punched him on the arm. He grinned at her and shook his head.

"Then what's the problem? If it gets messed up, and it's going to, just fix it." He shrugged and pulled her to him.

Of course it was no big deal to him. He was a man, so what did he know about a black women's hair? She was not a wash-and-go girl. Usually, when she washed her hair, it took her about two hours to wash, dry, and flat iron. She didn't have any of her supplies here, so she'd have to figure it out.

Later.

Wade closed the gap between them. Joy watched, fascinated, as his gray eyes darkened with lust.

"I won't have a choice," she murmured. She would have to do something to it later before it dried. She doubted he had a blow dryer around.

Wade swooped down and captured her lips with his. A moan slipped from him while his tongue immediately took control of the kiss.

It was quite easy to get lost in a kiss with Wade.

He bent down and hoisted her up. Her legs automatically wrapped around his waist as he walked into the shower. The warm air surrounded them, but Joy paid it no mind.

Her body was awakening to the feel of Wade pressed hard against her. The warm water ran down her back, and the thoughts of her hair were long forgotten.

The feeling of his long, firm shaft brushing on her filled her with excitement. Wade walked over and pushed her to the wall.

A gasp escaped her from the chill of the tiles.

Wade tore his mouth from hers and went on an exploration of his own. His lips moved up her jawline and down to her neck. She dove her fingers into his thick hair. The dark curls had been driving her crazy.

His body leaned into hers, crushing her breasts between them. The water skated over their bodies, and their hands slid easier.

Joy tightened her legs around Wade. She was amazed at how easily he was able to hold her up. He pressed hot kisses along her skin. Joy threw her head back to allow him to reach any part of her he so desired.

"I can't get enough of you," he murmured, his hand cupping her breast. It filled his entire hand while he massaged and played with the nipple.

Joy met Wade's intense gaze and didn't know what to say. It was the same for her. She'd loved every minute they had spent together.

Returning to his place, he had blown her mind. She had thought the electricity between them had been hot at the bowling alley.

She had misjudged it.

They had literally scorched the sheets. It was a

wonder the bed didn't catch fire. The sex between them was worthy of a ten-alarm fire.

Had the fire department arrived, there wouldn't have been any explanation they could have offered up.

"I'm not going anywhere," she admitted. It was the truth. There was something between them, and they would be fools to ignore it. Her heart raced while watching Wade lower his head to her.

The kiss was deep and sensual. His tongue took full advantage of her lips parting. It goaded Joy to come out and play.

Her body was heating up. The warmth from the shower was increasing her temperature. Her hair was plastered to her head, but she didn't care.

All she could think of was Wade.

He was filling her every thought. All the past fighting and arguing was just foreplay for what was to come. She understood that now. He'd get on her nerves, and she the same for him. It was a tale as old as time.

And currently, he was hers. She didn't know what the future was going to hold for them, but there was one thing she knew for certain.

She needed him inside her.

Her core clenched with need at the feel of his cock brushing against her.

"Is that so?"

Wade lined up his cock with her opening. Her muscles tensed when he surged forward. She released a cry at the sensation of his thick cock stretching her channel. He paused and brought her face to his. He covered her mouth again with his.

Joy groaned and rotated her hips. She craved a release from him. The loving he'd put on her the night before had her waiting for the next big orgasm.

"Whoa, there." He gripped her hips in his hands. "You keep that up, and this will be over sooner than it needs to be."

"What?" She flexed her inner muscles by doing a kegel, grinning playfully. "This?"

Wade growled and nipped her chin.

She squeezed again.

"You think you're funny." A teasing glint appeared in his eyes. He withdrew from her and thrust forward.

Joy released a grunt at how deep he went.

Oh boy.

Maybe she shouldn't have teased him so.

His strokes were long and sure. Joy hung on, clamping her arms around his neck.

Their eyes were locked together, and she couldn't look away if she tried. Her heart was pounding. She gripped his hair and brought him close to her. She trailed her tongue across his lips and tightened her fingers in his hair, holding his face to hers.

A shudder rippled through his body. Wade's lips parted to allow his groan to escape.

She ground her hips against him, her body moving in sync with the rhythm he set.

"Wade," she chanted.

He snatched her off the wall and brought her to him. Joy held on with her arms around his neck. She wasn't going to question the strength this man had to hold her up when the sensation of him sliding inside her was heavenly.

His thrusts became harder.

The air rushed from her lungs.

Wade Brooks was consuming her, and she didn't want it any other way.

Joy's eyes fluttered closed as an electric current rushed through her. Her orgasm was coming for her, and there was nothing to stop it.

She threw back her head, crying out as an intense climax overtook her.

Wade's hoarse yell followed her.

Their bodies slowed to a halt.

Still, he held her up as if she weighed nothing.

Her legs remained locked around him, as were her arms.

She leaned her head down and rested her forehead on his. The emotions rolling through her left her speechless.

His large hand roamed her back, sending chills through her body.

She opened her eyes and found him staring at her. She smiled and shook her head.

"Wade, this was..." She didn't know what to say. The man had worked her body in ways she'd only dreamed of.

"Perfect," his deep voice rumbled.

Her breath caught in her throat. She agreed. Today had been the best day she'd had in a long time.

She didn't know what this was between them, but she was determined to explore it. There was just one problem.

Her family.

"Y'all ain't going to find out the sex of the baby?"
Carson asked incredulously. He scratched his head
and turned to Parker with a confused look.

Wade, Carson, and Parker stood outside the corral
watching Tyler ride atop of Rocky. Wade observed his
nephew with pride. The kid had taken to riding a horse
just as he thought he would.

What Jonah Brooks had done was unforgivable.

Wade still couldn't believe the lengths his father
had gone to to keep Parker from Maddy. Had she not
moved back to Shady Springs, they may not even have
known Tyler existed.

"What are you hoping for?" Wade asked.

It would be nice to have a little Brooks girl running
around with pigtails. Jonah was one of four boys. Out
of all the Brooks cousins, there was only one girl.

"All we want is a healthy baby," Parker replied. He,
like his son, had on his beat-up Stetson. Tyler was the

spitting image of Parker. When Wade had first met Tyler, he couldn't stop looking at the child. Maddy had been so flustered and trying to leave that Wade hadn't asked any questions.

He wasn't shocked when it was revealed Tyler was Parker's son. It all made sense.

"If it's a girl, I say we go stock up on more ammunition," Wade teased.

Each of the Brooks brothers loved to shoot. It was a pastime of theirs. They were ranchers, and had to know how to use a gun. There were plenty of predatory animals out in the wild who tried to come onto the land to steal animals.

Parker visibly swallowed hard. Apparently, he hadn't thought of what having a girl would mean.

"Fuck, yeah. Y'all know how we were chasing girls when we were younger," Carson chuckled.

Wade joined in. Carson was speaking from experience. He'd been chased off a ranch before by a farmer with a gun.

"Shit," Parker cursed. He yanked off his hat and tunneled his trembling hand through his hair. He pushed his hat down onto his head and leaned against the fence. "They might as well bury me under the jail now."

Wade slapped Parker on his shoulder. "Don't worry, brother. We'll put aside bail money for you."

"Y'all remember when Uncle Henry caught Haley on her first date?" Carson snickered.

Their poor cousin was the only girl in another family of all boys. Her father, Henry, Jonah's brother, showed up at the party she was at with a shotgun and her three brothers.

"Damn, I had forgot about that." Parker scoffed.

Wade grinned. Haley and he were the same age. Wade had been at that party and almost died from laughter. His uncle and cousins hadn't dragged Haley away from the party. Oh no. They'd stayed and stood in the corner the entire time overseeing the date. Haley had rushed away, embarrassed.

"I wouldn't show up with a rifle." Parker sniffed. He scrubbed a hand along his face and shook his head. "Nope. I'll have my Glock in my holster."

"Parker!" Eliana called from the back door.

Parker released a deep sigh and turned, glancing over his shoulder. "Keep an eye on him. I have to go do payroll with Pa." He pushed off the fence with a look of dread on his face.

"Want me to do it?" Wade asked. Tensions were still there between Jonah and Parker. The day Jonah had the heart attack was the day everything had been revealed.

Wade had never seen such rage in his brother before. It had taken everything Carson and Wade had to keep Parker from getting his hands on Jonah. But after hearing the entire story, Wade sympathized with this brother. With the family business, it wasn't as if Parker could totally avoid their father.

Parker could have walked away from Blazing Eagle Ranch and started over, but this was his birthright, just as it was for Carson and Wade.

None of them could just walk away.

He and Carson tried to be a buffer between their brother and father.

"I'm good." Parker shook his head. "This shouldn't take long."

Parker spun on his heel and walked toward the house. Wade turned around and watched his brother. He couldn't even begin to fathom what was going through Parker's head whenever he looked Jonah in the eye.

Parker was one hell of a man to sit across from the person who had forever changed his life. Not that Jonah was one hundred percent to blame, but had he not interfered, Maddy, Parker, and Tyler's lives would have come out much differently.

"Hey, Eliana!" he called out.

Carson echoed out a greeting, too. Carson moved next to Wade and rested his foot on the fence.

Tyler and Rocky trotted over to them. Rocky was a wise, older horse Parker had found on a farm who practically gave him away when they heard it was for a child.

"Looking good, fellas," Wade praised.

"How am I doing, Uncle Wade?" Tyler asked, pushing back his hat. His eyes, the same as all the Brooks men, landed on Wade.

"You're doing well. I'm so proud of you, kid."

"Want to see a trick I taught Rocky?" Tyler's gaze darted between Carson and Wade.

"Of course. Show us what you got," Carson encouraged.

Wade loved his nephew as if he were his own son. It was good to have a youngster living on the ranch. Even though they had Kiddie Camp yearly, it was nothing like having Tyler there.

Wade hoped to one day have a son of his own.

Flashes of Joy's face when she'd climaxed came to mind. Their night together had been one he would never forget. He couldn't get enough of her. He'd lost track of how many times they had made love.

Her body had been warm, inviting, and so responsive to his.

Wade couldn't stop thinking about her. He'd only just taken her home a few hours earlier after they'd finally left the bedroom. He'd made them a late breakfast, and had managed to keep his hands to himself.

The kiss in the car almost had him pulling her over

and onto his lap, but he resisted.

Already, he was getting aroused thinking of their shower. Honestly, the plan was to just take a shower, but the second he'd got her in there, all thoughts left his brain. Seeing her naked curves lit a fire in him.

Wade blinked and focused on Tyler. He had to stop thinking of her, or he would be walking around with raging erection all day.

Rocky pranced away to the middle of the corral.

Tyler called out to Rashad, who had just arrived on horseback.

"What's up, buddy?" Rashad said, a hand who had worked for the ranch for years. He was a lead hand, and was very trustworthy. Rashad had grown up in Shady Springs, and was a few years older than Wade. They had gone to high school together, but Rashad had graduated before Wade.

Wade's curiosity was piqued. What was Tyler up to? His nephew guided Rocky around with his rope in his hands.

"I want to show them what I've been working on," Tyler replied.

Rashad's grin widened. Glancing over at Wade and Carson, he tipped his hat to them. "Be right back."

He trotted off, and disappeared around to the other side of the barn.

"I need to ask you something," Carson murmured.

"What's up, little brother?"

"Not that it's any of my business, but I saw you leaving this morning, and if I didn't know any better, I would have thought it was Joy Whitaker in your truck." Carson turned his curious gaze to him.

Wade froze. He hadn't thought anyone would have seen them. Not that he was trying to hide her.

"What if it was?"

"Makes no difference to me, but our families have been feuding since before any of us were born." Carson shrugged. "You sure that was a smart move?"

Wade skated a hand over his jaw and thought about it. The feud wasn't them. They didn't hate the Whitakers. They had grown up knowing of the feud, and naturally sided with their family.

He and Joy had their quarrels and arguments throughout the years. Even though there were times she got on his nerves, he had actually enjoyed it. Seeing her pissed off was the highlight of his days, but now, seeing her orgasm because of him was now his favorite pastime.

"Joy and I have buried the hatchet," Wade responded.

"Does Dad know?"

"None of his business," Wade snapped. He was a grown man, and didn't have to explain what he did or who he hung out with to his father.

They all knew what their father was capable of.

Jonah Brooks didn't need to know about everything going on in his sons' lives.

"Hey, don't get pissed at me. I just asked a question." Carson held his hands up. "What changed her mind? She always—you know what? Never mind. I don't want to know what you did to change her mind," Carson chuckled, shaking his head.

Wade snorted. "Get your mind out of the gutter."

His brother was smart, and he'd let him imagine what he wanted. It wasn't a secret about the Brooks brothers. They had a way with women, and that was how it had always been.

What it was, Wade didn't know.

Could it be their looks?

The money?

Cowboy life?

Women flocked to the three of them like flies on cow dung.

He remembered back in the day when he and Carson would go with Parker on the circuit. The buckle bunnies were out in full flock.

There was never a day there weren't women around.

But now, there was only one woman who was capturing Wade's attention.

There was no way in hell he would be sharing with

his brother the things that he and Joy had done together. There were just some things he did not speak about.

"There are plenty of things from the past that needed to be changed. New beginnings," he said.

Wade caught sight of a little calf Rashad had let loose in the corral. Wade tapped Carson on the shoulder and pointed. Rashad stood on the other side of the fence, laughing.

"Well, I'll be..." Carson cackled.

Tyler guided Rocky around. Concentration was on the kid's face as he raced after the calf. He and his horse moved as one. His rope was in the air, just as he had been taught. He swung it, and waited for the perfect time, while holding the extra length in his other hand.

Rocky picked up speed and was right behind the small cow. Tyler tossed his rope. Wade watched with bated breath as it landed around the cattle's neck.

Tyler pulled back on the rope, drawing it taut around the calf. They came to a halt. Tyler looked over at them, beaming.

Wade and Carson went wild, hooting, clapping, and whistling. Pride filled Wade. He had been working with Tyler on his lassoing for a while now. Apparently, his nephew had been practicing with Rashad. He was going to grow up to be one hell of a cowboy.

"What time did the sheep bring you home?" Georgy Whitaker asked.

Joy couldn't look her mother in the eye. They were out in the pasture, watching the dogs wrangle the sheep in.

It was time to rotate them in a different area. This was a common practice to make sure they didn't pick up any parasites that could be living in the earth.

The Whitakers took pride in raising their sheep, and worked with highly trained soil specialists to ensure the grass and land were safe for the sheep. The animals were sold for top-grade meat, and everything had to be perfect for the animals.

Joy gave a loud whistle, commanding the dogs. One thing she loved about sheep was that they were smart. If they were scared, they would stick together to try and get away from a threat.

At the moment, the dogs were the threat to the sheep.

Lacie, the leader of the dogs, did her job in helping the other two get the sheep moved. The flock rushed into the area where Joy wanted them. She jogged over and shut the gate.

"Good job, guys." She rubbed Lacey, Minnie, and Duke on their heads. The dogs lived for getting praised for a job well done. They barked and yipped, begging for her hand to run over their heads.

Joy stood to her full height and caught her mother standing with her hands on her hips. The dogs continued to bark and ran around her in circles.

"What?" Joy asked, unsure as to why her mother was staring at her.

"Spill it, young lady."

Joy rolled her eyes. She may be thirty years old, but her mother had her feeling like a sixteen-year-old schoolgirl.

"I went out," she mumbled.

"With who? When your father and I got home last night, you were gone." They fell in step with each other as they walked back to the barn.

The dogs ran ahead, yipping and barking.

Joy shrugged. "A friend."

"Joy Amanda Whitaker," Georgy practically growled.

Joy winced. If her mother called her by her full name, then she was in trouble.

"Okay! I was out with Wade."

Georgy paused and gawked at her. Joy stopped walking and turned back to face her.

"Wade Brooks. As in, Jonah Brookses son?"

Joy bit her lip. She knew she should not have shared the truth. She already knew what was going to come next.

"Yeah," Joy replied.

"Are you trying to give your father a heart attack? You know the history of our families, and you went out with a Brooks?"

"It wasn't Wade's fault, or mine." She didn't want to explain her actions, but she had no choice. Between her parents, Georgy was the more rational one. If she could get her mom on her side, then she would have fighting chance with her father.

Joy liked Wade. A lot. It wasn't just the mind-blowing sex. Well, it was a big part of it, but she liked the way he made her feel when they were together. The way they laughed with each other, shared the same humor, were competitive.

She wanted to see him again. She didn't know where this was going between them, but she was all in to see.

"Mom, Wade and I came to a truce."

"A truce?" Georgy gasped and stepped away from Joy with wide eyes. "Let me get this right. You stayed out all night with the son of the man who refused to sell back the land they took from us? Doing what?"

Joy covered her face with her hands. She knew the story about Jonah. Turning around, she removed her hands to face her mother and froze.

Did she tell the truth?

Or did she lie?

Joy was never one to fib. At the moment, with the fierce gaze her mom was giving her, Georgy would know.

"Mom, you have to trust that I know what I'm doing," she pleaded.

"It's not you I don't trust. You have a big heart, Joy Whitaker. I don't want to see you hurt."

"I'll be fine." Joy tucked her thick hair behind her ear.

Why was Wade being punished for his father's past doings? He was his own man, and a trustworthy one at that. In all the years she'd known him, she'd given him shit, and he gave it right back to her.

Their rivalry hadn't been a vindictive one.

Wade had never done anything to her that would truly make her hate him.

Joy would just have to make her family see what she saw in Wade.

"Here are my two favorite women." Her father's deep voice rang out from the barn. Davis Whitaker, Sr. was a tall, wiry man, with smooth, medium-almond skin. His smile was genuine, and his laugh was one that could make the hardest of men crack a smile.

Davis was a hard worker, and proud of the ranch he owned. Sheep farming wasn't as glamorous as cattle ranching was made out to be, but it was rewarding.

Davis put his blood, sweat, and tears into the land his ancestors passed down to him. He had raised his children to have a love for the family business. Joy couldn't see herself doing anything else. Ranching and raising sheep were in her blood.

Her brother, Junior, walked along with their father. He was the spitting image of Senior, with the same build, and even his walk. Her brother was said to be the mirror image of her father at his current age.

The dogs ran to her father and brother, begging for attention. Not that they were starved for affection or anything. The three of them just happened to be attention snobs.

Senior and Junior had no choice but to rub the dogs' heads and greet them.

Joy's heart raced. Now was not the time for her to tell her father about Wade.

Not yet.

She didn't know when, but she would find the right

time. And Junior? She didn't know how he would take it. He was a stubborn alpha male who was fiercely protective of her.

When she was younger, he was the one who had chaperoned her meetups with friends at school sporting events. No one dared mess with her if her bulldog of a brother was around.

Junior was even worse than her father when it came to their neighbors. He had no love for anyone who carried the last name Brooks.

"You are going to tell him," Georgy announced in a low voice.

Joy focused her attention on Georgy. She jerked her head in a nod. She didn't want to engage her mom at this point.

"Not now. There's nothing to tell." Joy turned away from her mother and watched her father approach them. She prayed Georgy remained silent.

"How are you, baby?" Davis placed a kiss on her forehead. He squeezed her shoulders and stared down at her.

"I'm good, Daddy. How are you?" she asked. Her arms immediately went around her father's waist. No matter how old she was, she was never too old to show her love for him. She was Daddy's girl, and she wasn't ashamed to admit it. Davis ensured that their childhood had been full of love, affection, and good times.

Her dad's strength was comforting. Joy released him and took a step back.

"Better now that I get to see your beautiful faces." Laughing, he moved from her to her mother. He wrapped his arm around her and dropped a hard kiss on her lips. "And I'm feeling really good now."

"Oh, you hush up, Davis." Georgy swatted Senior on the chest. She flushed like a young schoolgirl.

Joy rolled her eyes and turned to her brother.

"What's up, sis?" Junior asked. He gently shoved her with his elbows.

"Nothing." She pushed back with a laugh.

The dogs were back to yipping and running around their feet, wanting to get in on the sibling shoving match. Joy giggled and jumped back as they tried to get in between her and Junior.

"Where have you two been?" Georgy asked. She leaned into her husband's embrace. It was a beautiful sight to see a couple who had been together as long as her parents and still be in love with each other. It was as if they were still in the honeymoon stage of their marriage.

"We went out to meet with the new owner of Reynolds' Meats," Senior replied.

Joy's interest was piqued by this. The company was a large meat processing company that had undergone a change in ownership. The Whitakers had done business with the Reynolds' for years. Her father had been worried that with the change in ownership, it would prove to be an issue.

"We needed to meet with them about our contracts, and if they will still honor what the last owners agreed upon," Junior chimed in. He wrapped his arm around Joy's shoulder.

"I have a good feeling about this year. The amount of lambs were up, and that will be a bonus," Senior announced, his grin wide.

"Davis, honey, that is amazing," Georgy gushed.

"I want to take everyone out to dinner. Lexi will be home tonight, and we can celebrate the Whitakers' good fortune." Senior's face was relaxed and carefree.

Joy smiled, proud of what her father had done with the ranch. It had prospered under his leadership.

Senior motioned for them to head up to the house.

"Time to celebrate. Make sure you put on your fancy duds for this," Junior cackled. He squeezed her shoulder and jogged off to catch up with their father. The dogs took off after him, vying for the Whitaker men's attention.

Georgy turned back and shot Joy a look, and she tried to ignore it. Her parents walked holding hands.

Joy fell behind them. Tonight was definitely not the time to tell her father who she had gone out with. Tonight was for Whitakers. They would go out together for a nice dinner and enjoy each other's company.

With her sister coming into town, that would take some heat off. Everyone's attention would be on her younger sister. Joy loved her, and it had been a few weeks since she had gotten to see her. They spoke on the phone frequently, but it was never the same as being in the same room together.

Even though they were five years apart, they were the best of friends. Lexi lived in the big city, and always came home with crazy stories.

Lost in thought, Joy almost missed the vibration of her phone in her back pocket. She pulled it out and saw a text from Wade.

Thinking about you.

She couldn't help the silly grin that spread across her face. What did she say back? Of course she had been thinking of Wade nonstop since he had dropped her off at home earlier.

The memory of his deep voice whispering in her ear sent a shiver down her spine. The feeling of his body pressed against hers was etched in her brain. If she closed her eyes and breathed in deeply, she could still smell his scent.

Wade Brooks had certainly done a number on her.

Joy glanced up and caught her mother looking over

her shoulder at her. She erased her smile and broke the stare.

I hope it's all good thoughts.

That was a safe reply. She didn't want to sound too desperate or "thirsty," as her sister would say.

"What's got you all smiling?" Junior asked.

Joy shook her head and put her phone back in her pocket. They arrived at the house. Her parents had disappeared inside. Junior stood by the door, holding it open for her.

"Oh, nothing. A friend sent me a stupid meme."

She walked up the stairs and stepped inside. Her phone vibrated again, and she ignored it.

She would have to make time for Wade later.

Much later.

"This was not a good idea," Carson mumbled.

"What were we supposed to do? Tell him no?" Wade stood outside the truck and scratched his head. He ran a hand through his hair, unsure of how they got into this situation.

"We could have ordered it to-go." Carson opened the tailgate and pulled out their father's wheelchair. Jonah had demanded to get out of the house. Ever since he had been released from the rehabilitation facility, he had been cooped up inside.

Wade felt sorry for him. Jonah had been a very independent man before the heart attack. Lately, he had been just as grouchy and a pain in the ass, but the longer he remained restricted to the house, the worse he got.

Wade had suggested they go out to dinner. He hadn't thought his father would actually take him up on the offer.

But Jonah agreed.

He even appeared excited to be going out to the popular restaurant. They had been shocked, but it was a win.

"We'll be fine," Wade assured his younger brother.

"I can't deal with all the bitching," Carson groaned. He placed the chair on the ground, while Wade shut the tailgate.

"Between the two of us, we can deal with the old man." Wade knew it was hard for his younger brother. He and Parker had shielded Carson as much as they could while growing up. Eliana only came during the week. At night, and on the weekends, they were on their own with helping their father. Wade started to wonder if he could offer Eliana extra money to come more often. There was just something about her that Jonah responded to.

Jonah was getting stronger, but Wade and Carson took turns spending the night up in the main house with him, not trusting to leave him by himself in the evening. Parker had his hands full with his family, and quite frankly, Wade didn't think it was best for their older brother to stay in the house alone with their father.

With as thick as the tension was between them, Wade didn't want to risk it exploding again.

"Come on. Let's go in. It looks like it's getting

packed in there." Wade walked up to the passenger door and opened it.

"I don't need that damn wheelchair," their father's voice rang out.

Carson rolled his eyes. Wade stared at Jonah, taking in his infamous scowl.

"It's to help you," Wade stated matter-of-factly.

"I had a heart attack. Ain't nothing wrong with my legs." Jonah pushed open the door.

"But Pa," Wade groaned. He really didn't want to sit out here in the parking lot and argue with the old man. Jonah was one stubborn son of a bitch, and they could be out here for hours until he got his way.

Wade glanced at Carson and jerked his head toward the trunk. Carson threw up his hands in exasperation. He began putzing with the chair to close it back up.

"The restaurant ain't that far. I can walk," Jonah muttered. He glared at Wade as if to challenge him.

Wade swept a hand across his face, and the fight escaped him.

"Fine, Pa. Just take it easy." Carson came to stand beside Wade.

They assisted him out of the truck, with Jonah shaking their hands off of him.

Jonah was a proud man, and Wade knew there was no way in hell his father would want to appear weak in public. He stood to his full height, and with slow, steady steps, made his way toward the building.

"You fall on your face, I'm not picking you up," Carson snorted before jogging ahead to open the door for them.

"Don't let me fall," Jonah retorted. He walked through the door and paused in front of Carson. "Smartass."

Wade's gaze met his brother's, and he bit back a chuckle at the widening of his eyes. What did he expect? Wade followed his father, with Carson pulling up the rear.

"Hello, fellas! Welcome to the Notorious C.O.W." The hostess greeted them with a warm smile. "I'm Renee. Is it the three of you?"

"Yes, ma'am." Wade positioned himself on one side of Jonah, with Carson on the other side.

"Give me a second." She glanced down at something on the podium before turning her attention to them. "It'll be a fifteen-minute wait."

"Don't let it be too long." Jonah leaned on Wade, putting on an Oscar-worthy performance. "I just got out of the hospital and wanted a really good meal."

Her eyes widened, and she nodded. "I'll be right back. Let me verify this other table is open."

She scurried away and into the dining area.

Wade had to keep his mouth from dropping open

as he watched her rush away. His father eyed him and winked. Carson snorted and looked away.

Wade took in the place. It had been a while since he'd eaten at the popular barbecue restaurant. It was owned and operated by David Walker, who had moved from Texas about ten years ago. The food was legendary around these parts.

Wade wasn't sure what they did while cooking the food, but it was damn good.

Tonight, almost every table was taken. The servers were bustling through the dining area, taking care of the customers.

Renee returned, holding a few menus in her arms. "Okay, fellas. I have the perfect table for you. Follow me."

Carson slapped Jonah on his shoulder. "Let's go, Pa. You lead the way."

They followed Renee to a table located in the corner, giving them a perfect view of the establishment.

"You boys are going to learn one day," Jonah chortled.

"Whatever, old man. They would have seated us soon," Carson quipped.

Wade reached for the menu, not wanting to engage with his father. He'd let Carson bicker with him. He was starving, and wanted to find out what the specials were.

"Howdy, fellas." A cute brunette stopped by their table. She was of medium build, and dressed in the restaurant's uniform of a T-shirt with a pig on the front, and jeans. She had a pretty smile, and was eyeing Carson. "I'm Faith, and I'll be your server tonight."

"Well hello, Faith." Wade smiled at her. "Busy night?"

"It's only just begun." She laughed. "What can I get you to drink?"

They placed their orders for drinks and appetizers with her. She scribbled down their request.

"Do you want to go ahead and order your dinner now?' she asked.

"Not yet. I'm still looking," Jonah replied, focusing on the menu.

"That's fine." Faith nodded. "Y'all take your time. I'll go put in your appetizers and grab your drinks in the meanwhile."

She smiled one last time at Carson before walking away.

"Looks like someone has her eye on you," Jonah remarked, peeking over the menu at Carson.

Carson glanced down at his own. "Whatever. Your eyes need to be checked."

Wade shook his head and turned back to view the specials.

They struck up a conversation with their father about the ranch, from the amount of new calves born, to a new fertilizer Wade wanted to order and try out.

"So, what all did you get at the auction?" Jonah sat back and asked.

"I got a new tractor for a decent price. Carson's been tinkering with it, and should have it up and running soon." Wade took a sip of his beer then set it back down. He had been able to get the one he had been eyeing for a good price.

"It's a beauty. I gave it a full tune-up and got it purring like a kitten," Carson declared. "We can start using it now."

"Your drinks," Faith announced. She stood near the table and placed their tall frosted mugs filled with beer down. "Appetizers should be up in a minute. Can I take your order now?"

Wade glanced around, and his father and Carson nodded. Faith left again after taking their orders. Wade watched his brother's head swivel in the direction Faith had disappeared in.

"I think Pa's eyes are just fine," Wade teased.

Carson's head flew back to them. A sheepish expression came over him. He leaned back in and laughed.

"Okay, maybe I'm interested." Carson shrugged, reaching for his beer.

"I knew what I was talking about," Jonah bragged.

Wade smiled at his brother and father. Hopefully, this outing would help Jonah feel as close to normal as possible.

Even if he was a pain in the ass most of the time.

Jonah laughed along with Carson and sipped his beer, looking the most relaxed Wade had seen him in a while.

Hell, he couldn't even remember the last time he and his brothers just sat around drinking with the old man. He was going to bask in the light atmosphere and pretend for a moment that everything with the family was fine.

Faith returned with their appetizers, and they immediately dug in. Jokes and great conversation went around the table. Wade was shocked that he was enjoying himself with his father and brother.

A party not too far from them broke out in a fit of laughter. Wade casually glanced over in that direction, his gaze landing on a familiar family having a great time.

The Whitakers.

Joy and her family were all smiles as they ate their dinner. Wade couldn't take his eyes off her. Memories of their night together surfaced.

He could still taste her on his tongue.

The sounds of her whimpers and cries of passion echoed in his head.

"Who you staring at, boy?" Jonah's voice broke through Wade's thoughts.

He turned around and found his father's eyes set on him.

"Oh, nothing. I see our neighbors, the Whitakers, are over there enjoying supper."

Jonah rotated slightly in his chair, then rotated back. "Hmph."

Wade reached for his mug and took another sip. He watched Joy get up from the table and head off toward the ladies' room.

"How about a drink from the bar? My treat," Wade offered.

"Whiskey," Jonah and Carson answered simultaneously.

"Like father, like son," Carson snickered.

"Coming up." Wade pushed back from the table and made his way through the busy restaurant, heading over to the bar. He placed his order and leaned back against the counter. The bartenders were swamped, but Wade was in no hurry.

He had the perfect spot to see Joy when she exited.

His heart raced as he waited for her.

A few minutes later, she emerged from the

restroom.

Apparently, she didn't see him standing there.

"Joy," he called out.

She jumped and spun around to him. Her eyes widened, and a small smile appeared on her lips.

Joy came to stand by him. "What are you doing here?"

He couldn't help but stare at her. She was beautiful, dressed in a shirt, tight jeans, and sandals.

"Carson and I got the old man out of the house, and figured we'd take him out to dinner. You?"

She glanced over at Jonah and Carson before facing him. "How is your father doing? They said he almost died."

"Yeah, it would take more than a heart attack to kill that son of a bitch," he muttered.

She leaned close to him.

"Aren't you the dutiful son, bringing Dad out for dinner." Her cheeky grin widened as she nudged him.

He loved her flirtatious nature. Where had this been all these years? If he had known the attraction was mutual between them, he would have acted on it years ago.

Wade had to admit, seeing her all riled up and fighting with her was a nice form of foreplay. If the sex continued to be as explosive, he would have to think of something to piss her off.

"Well, it was either dinner at a restaurant, or push him out in the woods and let nature take its course," he joked.

"You wouldn't!" She shoved him slightly in a playful manner.

"Here's your drinks, sir. Three whiskey straights." The bartender placed the three glasses on the counter.

"Thanks, man." Wade turned and tossed a few bills onto the counter.

The guy scooped up the bills and gave him a salute then scurried off to help a few other customers.

Wade picked up a glass and offered it to Joy. "Have a drink with me."

Joy bit her lip and looked over at her family. Wade followed her gaze and noticed her mother was watching at them. Wade nodded to Mrs. Whitaker before returning his attention to Joy.

"What the hell," she muttered, snatching the glass from him.

"Attagirl." Wade picked up one and signaled to the bartender for another.

"Here you are," Carson announced, his grin wide. He slapped Wade on the shoulder. "Joy Whitaker. How the hell are you?"

"I'm good, Carson. How about yourself?" Joy asked.

Carson twisted toward Wade with his eyebrows

raised. "I'm doing wonderful."

Wade already knew there was going to be an inter-rogation later.

"Pop sent me to find out what was taking so long."

Joy's smile faltered, and Wade bit back a curse. They hadn't really spoken about what this was between them, or if they were going to go public with it. Wade wanted to explore this and see where it ended up. He was getting up in age, and playing the field wasn't as fun as it was when he was in his early twenties. He was now thirty, and had to admit that his father was right about one thing.

It was time to settle down.

"Another whiskey." The barkeep stopped back and dropped off the glass.

"Thanks." Wade slid another bill across the counter and motioned for Carson to take the glasses, nodding toward their table.

Carson got the message loud and clear. He winked at Wade and snatched them up.

"See ya later, Joy." Carson nodded to Joy and headed back to the table.

Wade sighed. "Don't mind Carson. I think he took too many hits to the head when he played football."

"I have a brother too, so I know how they are."

They held up their glasses and clinked them together.

"New beginnings," Wade said softly.

Joy tilted her head to the side and stared at him. "New beginnings."

Wade knocked back his drink and ignored the burn of the amber liquid. He had eyes only for Joy. The smooth span of her neck brought back memories of his lips trailing kisses along it. He had a flashback of his face pressed into the crook of her neck when he'd been over her, thrusting deep inside her.

Joy's name being called broke through his carnal thoughts.

One night of Joy wouldn't be enough.

She turned at the sound and placed her glass back on the counter.

"I gotta go," she said, her eyes filled with uncertainty.

"I'll call you later, once I get Pa home and settled," he promised. He didn't want to let her go, but he had to.

"You better." She spun around, walking away from him.

Wade's gaze dropped down to her ample ass, and he was unashamed to be looking it over.

Damn, she has a sexy bottom.

He pushed off the bar and headed back to his table. His mind was made up.

Joy Whitaker would be his.

13

Joy walked back to her family, her heart beating erratically. Wade had her stomach in knots. It had taken
everything in her not to lean in and kiss him. She just
wanted to feel his arms wrapped around her.

A warmness washed over her.

How could a man be that damn sexy?

Just seeing him brought back every memory of his
hands, lips, and tongue on her. Her cheeks grew hot
with the personal knowledge of what Wade Brooks
was known for.

Maybe it was the whiskey.

Taking shots hadn't been the plan, but one look at
her mother staring at her had Joy tossing caution in the
wind.

She blinked a few times, trying to concentrate on
walking.

Damn alcohol. Thank goodness she rode with her
family.

She arrived back at the table and ignored the stares. Her parents, sister, and brother enjoyed their dinner that had come while she'd stepped away. They had already demolished the appetizers.

"Having a drink with the enemy, eh?" her father chuckled.

"What did Wade want?" Junior asked. His gaze zeroed in on her with his glass paused in midair.

"Just a friendly neighbor drink." She shrugged and tried to act nonchalant.

"You sure about that?" Georgy asked, raising her eyebrows. Her mother was not going to get off her back until she came clean to her father about her relationship with Wade.

Joy grew uncomfortable as everyone turned to her.

"I wouldn't mind a little attention from Wade Brooks," Lexi snorted.

Her sister had arrived an hour before they had left for dinner. Her younger sister would be late to her own funeral, not having any concept of time. Lexi was a shade lighter than Joy, but they were always confused as twins. Her hair was dark and long, falling past her shoulders.

"Lexi Whitaker!" her mother gasped.

"What?" Lexi's eyes grew wide. "Well, they may be the enemy, but the Brooks brothers are hot."

Joy rolled her eyes at her sister. Lexi always spoke

her mind, and her family never said anything. If it were Joy who came straight out and said something like that, it would have been a different thing.

Her family struck up a conversation, while Joy began digging into her lamb chops. She relaxed slightly as her family appeared to return to normal.

Joy tried not to stare over at Wade's table, but she couldn't help it. He sat with Carson and his father. Jonah Brooks looked as if he'd aged a little. The entire town had heard of him getting sick and being hospitalized.

Living in a small town, everyone knew everything about everyone. It was a gift and a curse. No secret was safe in Shady Springs.

Joy would never wish anything bad on anyone, but she hoped he was a changed man. She noticed Parker was missing. The rumor around town was that he was engaged to Maddy King. Turned out her child was Parker's, and now they were getting married and expecting again.

Joy remembered Maddy from when they were in high school. Maddy had been a year behind Joy. Maddy had been a quiet, good girl. Her father had been known as the town drunk, and Joy recalled feeling sorry for her.

Her siblings' laughter broke through her thoughts.

"So, tell us, Lexi. What's new with your job?" Junior probed.

"I'm so glad you asked," Lexi replied. She reached for her drink and took a sip. Her grin widened as she bounced in her seat. "One of the reasons I came home was to share that I was just promoted."

"That's awesome," Joy gushed.

Cheers went around the table. Joy was extremely happy for her sister. It couldn't have happened to a better person.

"Baby, I knew you would go far," their father announced.

Georgy hugged Lexi with tears spilling down her cheeks. Their mother was an emotional wreck when it came to her children's success.

"Tell us. What are you going to be doing now?" Georgy asked.

It was no surprise that Lexi was moving up in her company. She was brilliant, and had graduated at the top of her class in college. She was a social media marketing genius who had designed ads similar to the television ads, but for the internet.

Lexi had worked hard from the moment she'd gotten the position at the firm. Joy knew of the long hours her sister had put in to make a name for herself. She was a Whitaker, so it was a given that she was a hard worker.

"I'm the new project manager, and now have a small team of four people working under me. Due to the boom in online advertising, I'm charged with expanding the department."

"I'm so proud of you kids." Senior wrapped an arm around Georgy and brought her in close. "We did good, Momma. Our ranch is prospering due to the diligence of this family. Joy and Junior have helped push it to what it is today. Our baby girl has a fancy job in the city. What else could we ask for?"

Tears teetered on the edge of Joy's eyelids. She took her glass and raised it in the air. Her family did the same, clinking them together.

"Now, all we need is to get our land back from the Brooks," Junior said.

Joy paused with her glass on her lips. She didn't know what to say. There just couldn't be one night where there wasn't talk of the Brooks family. Joy fought back rolling her eyes. She was so tired of it.

Why couldn't her brother and father just move on?

Could they really hate Jonah and his family forever?

"Hear, hear." Senior raised his glass again before finishing off his beer.

Joy ignored her mother's gaze. She faked a cough and took a sip of her Coke. She put on a smile and sighed.

"Good evening, Whitakers."

Joy glanced up and froze. Jonah had the nerve to be standing at their table. His breaths were coming a little fast, but he stood tall with his sons behind him.

"Jonah, Wade, Carson," Senior greeted them.

The brothers murmured their greeting and nodded to everyone at the table.

Joy's eyes were wide in shock. What did Jonah want?

"I hope y'all are enjoying your meal tonight. I don't want to take up much of your time. I just wanted to come be neighborly and say hello."

The entire table fell silent.

This was a first.

Usually, Jonah snarled and cursed whenever spoken to.

Her parents shared a look before turning back to Jonah.

"Well, that is mighty nice of you, Jonah. How have you been doing? Heard you had some heart issues," her father said.

"Yeah, it would take more than a heart attack to take me out." Jonah unconsciously rubbed his chest. "But I'm doing much better now."

Joy's attention moved to Wade. His eyes were locked on hers. He broke the stare and casually pulled his phone from his pocket. She quickly studied his soft cotton shirt and the way it molded to his hardened physique.

Her breath caught in her throat remembering the feel of his chest, and the soft curls of hair underneath her fingers. Her core clenched, thinking of what they had done to each other.

Her back pocket vibrated.

"Well, I need to head home. I may have overdone it tonight. Being in the house all the time was making me stir crazy, and dinner was just what I needed." Jonah tipped his head to them and waved as he walked off.

"Goodnight," she murmured along with her family. Joy smiled softly at the Brooks men. She didn't miss the wink Wade threw her.

Her heart stuttered as she watched him stride away. His gentle nature and how he stayed back to ensure his father made it through the restaurant wasn't lost on her.

Jesus, the man just kept getting sexier.

Her eyes were glued to him until she could no longer see him.

A firm kick landed on her shin. Joy jumped, and found Lexi staring at her with a raised eyebrow.

"Girl," Lexi mouthed, a devilish grin on her lips.

Joy groaned internally and shook her head. She knew she was going to have some explaining to do when she got home.

Her parents and brother were too busy chatting about the recent encounter.

"Maybe being in the coma did something to him," Georgy muttered.

"Well, they say near-death experiences can change a man," Senior replied.

"Maybe he got a little taste of Hell and got a new look on life." Junior huffed.

Joy's gaze flew to her brother. He was never one to bite his tongue. Whatever he thought, it came out. His hatred toward the Brooks family was evident.

"Junior!" Georgy gasped. She clutched her chest and narrowed her eyes on him. "I don't ever want to hear you talk like that. He may be a nasty old man, but we will not wish Hell on anyone. We are not to judge."

Junior rolled his eyes. "You have to admit, something is up. That man doesn't know how to be neighborly or cordial," he remarked.

"The boy has a point," their father chuckled.

"I hope you don't mind, but I want to go meet some friends later," Lexi announced, changing the subject. "I need a ride. Can you drop me off over Karin's house?"

"Sure." Joy nodded and pulled her phone out. She couldn't wait any longer to see the messages waiting on her.

Swiping the screen, she saw a new text from Wade. *Hey, sexy lady. How about I pick you up instead?*

She bit her lip to keep from giggling like a schoolgirl.

My sister needs me to take her somewhere. How about I meet you?

"You girls have fun," Georgy called out behind Joy and Lexi.

Joy bit her lip and prayed her mother didn't come out onto the porch. The door banged shut. Her prayer was not answered.

"Thanks, Mom. See you later." Lexi turned around and waved as they walked toward Joy's truck. "I'll try not to stay out too late."

Joy muttered a curse.

"Joy, what about you? Will the sheep be bringing you home again?" Georgy asked.

Joy closed her eyes and paused. She breathed in deeply, spinning to face her mother. She plastered on a smile and hoped there weren't a ton of questions.

"I'm not sure. Don't wait up." Joy blew her a kiss and laughed.

Georgy's eyebrows rose sharply. She folded her arms and shook her head.

"Come on, sis," Lexi said. She wrapped her arm around Joy's shoulders and pulled her toward the car.

"You are telling me everything," she whispered in Joy's ear.

They arrived at the truck and got in. Georgy was still standing on the porch, watching them while Joy started the engine and drove away.

"Why do I feel like I'm going to be in trouble when I return home?" Joy muttered. The truck flew down the dirt road leading to the main one.

"Okay. Out with it," Lexi demanded.

"Bossy," Joy murmured. She had to fight to keep the smile from overtaking her. What could she tell her sister that was rated PG?

"So, you and Wade?" Lexi asked incredulously.

Joy glanced over at Lexi and found her waiting for a reply.

She shrugged. "It sort of happened."

"And Mom knows?"

"Yes," Joy groaned. She tightened her hands on the wheel. She slowed the vehicle down so she could turn onto the highway. "You know that woman has interrogation skills that would rival the CIA."

Lexi let down her window. Joy did the same to allow the warm summer air in. It felt good to get something about Wade off her chest.

"Don't think you are getting out of telling me the dirty details." Lexi elbowed her slightly.

Joy giggled and shook her head. She wasn't spilling any details.

"Is it true about the Brooks brothers?"

"What have you heard?" Joy gasped. She looked over at her sister, who sat with her arms folded, and her lips twisted up in a smirk.

"How can I not hear? You do realize we are from Shady Springs, Colorado, where secrets don't exist," Lexi cackled.

"I don't kiss and tell." Joy raised her chin. She was a lady, and did not share her sexual exploits with people, especially not her younger sister.

"So there was kissing?" Lexi shoved her with her elbow again. "You are such a prude. At least tell me, was he good in bed? Left you walking bowlegged? Rearranged your insides?"

Joy rolled her eyes. What was up with this younger generation? They were only five years apart, but sometimes, Joy felt ancient compared to Lexi.

But if she didn't share something with her pesky sibling, Joy would never hear the end of it.

"Let's just say, after I drop you off, I'm heading straight to his house, and I do not plan to come home."

Lexi howled and danced in her seat. Joy burst out laughing at her sister's antics. She loved when Lexi came home. No one in the house would understand what Joy was going through. Lexi always had an open mind and never judged.

That was what she loved about her sister.

"Calm down," Joy said.

"How can I? My sister is banging the very fine Wade Brooks."

"Lexi Whitaker!" Joy exclaimed.

"Saving a horse, riding a cowboy, are we?" Lexi had tears streaming down her face.

Joy shook her head, but couldn't hold back the laughter. Her sister was crazy, and if she didn't know any better, Lexi must have pregamed before leaving the house.

"Who all is going out with y'all?" Joy asked, trying to change the subject.

Lexi settled back and calmed down. "Karin, Toi, Nora, and Rasheeda," she rattled off.

"Girls' night." Joy wagged her eyebrows at Lexi.

"I would ask if you want to come, but I'm sure a dick appointment outweighs girls' night any day!"

"Lexi!"

Wade tore his mouth from Joy's. He hadn't been able to stop thinking about her the second he'd stepped out of the restaurant. Just the sight of her brought up the intense attraction he had for her.

The minute he'd dropped off Carson and his father at the main house, he'd sped home to ready his place for her. He needed to tidy up his living room before she arrived.

His doorbell had rung. He'd opened the door, and before he knew it, she'd taken two steps into his house when he'd practically pounced on her.

Wade stared down into Joy's big brown orbs. His heart raced, and his cock was drilling a hole in his pants, demanding to be released.

"Joy, I don't know what you do to me," he admitted. He held her face in his hands and slid his thumb over her smooth skin. It was the God's honest truth. He had never had this strong of a reaction to someone.

Her gaze dropped down to his waist, then returned to his. Her swollen lips spread into a wide grin.

"I can sort of guess what I do to you," she quipped.

She pressed against his erection, eliciting a growl from him.

He swooped down and kissed her again. This time, it wasn't gentle.

Her moan echoed through the air, and it fanned the fire of his desire for her. His brain was a scrambled mess, and he was being led by his other head.

He was desperate to feel her moist channel wrapped around him. A shudder passed through him with the anticipation of being balls deep inside of her.

Just the thought of being inside her again had him flattening her against the door.

Joy's fingers threaded into his hair and gripped the strands tight. He ignored the stinging pain as she held on to him. He tilted his head to the side and deepened the kiss.

He dropped his hands down to the edge of her shirt and lifted it up. The kiss was interrupted for a brief moment as they worked together to rid themselves of their shirts.

"You're so fucking beautiful," Wade murmured, taking her in. As always, her breasts were encased in fancy lingerie. This time in a bright-pink bra that did little to hide her dark areolae and beaded nipples. He reached up and cupped her mounds, rubbing her nipples.

"You make me feel beautiful with the way you look at me," she whispered.

He paused, flicking his gaze to hers. He was shocked by her words.

Didn't she know how gorgeous she was?

How could she not?

There was no way on God's green earth that Joy Whitaker didn't know she was the total package.

Beautiful, brains, and a certified cowgirl.

"Darlin', everything about you is downright sexy." He slid his hand up to her neck and brought her closer to him. He covered her mouth with his, giving her a deep, passionate kiss. He wanted her to know exactly how he felt about her.

Soon, both of them were naked, with a pile of clothes resting on the floor around them. There would be no time to rush into the bedroom. Wade's stiff cock would make walking almost unimaginable. He groaned and hitched a hand behind her knee, hefting her up against the door again, allowing his weight to keep her there safely.

Joy automatically wrapped her legs around him, locking her ankles together. She pressed close to him, nipping his chin, and leaving a trail of kisses along his jawline.

"Wade," she moaned. Her hands dove into his hair again as their lips connected.

He couldn't get enough of the taste of her.

Wade's body was heating up. Every touch, moan, and caress of her hands on him was sending tremors through him.

He was blown away by their connection.

Who would have known they had so much chemistry?

Deep inside him, there was a fierce ache to claim her, to make her his. He didn't know where this urge came from, but he liked it.

He didn't want any other man to think she was available. He'd caught the stares of the men in the restaurant looking at her while she'd walked through it.

That had riled something in him. He had wanted to march over to each table and issue a stern warning that she was off the market.

She was his, and he wanted the entire world to know.

"Damn, Joy. I need to be inside you." His voice was strained. He was trying to control himself, and not go barbaric on her.

Joy ran her hands over his shoulders, kneading the taut muscles. Her small hands landed on his face. She cupped his jaw and smiled at him.

"Take me, Wade. Make me yours." Her breasts were crushed between them.

He held her up against the door and used his other hand to guide the blunt tip of his cock to her entrance.

He groaned. Her labia was slick with her sweet honey. It coated the head of his cock, and he could have wept with how wet she was.

Her body was so responsive to his.

Her folds parted as he pressed forward. Wade held her steady while he slid inch by inch inside her, until he was completely buried in her channel.

Wade refused to take his eyes off her face. Her eyes were closed, and her lips were parted. If he could describe the reaction of ecstasy, he would say it was written all over her face.

He grew harder watching her.

He held still at first, allowing her to adjust to his size. Her inner muscles contracted around him. He wasn't sure if she had done it on purpose, or if it was an automatic response, but he loved it.

Wade stirred, no longer able to hold still. He gripped her legs firmly as she wrapped her arms tighter around his neck.

"Yes," Joy hissed.

She threw her head back, giving him access to her neck. He lowered his head and trailed kisses over the smooth expanse of skin. He nipped it, but then soothed it with his tongue.

He drove deeper inside with each thrust. Her gasps and moans were driving him insane.

They moved together. Joy rotated her hips against his, allowing him to slide farther inside her. He gasped, thrusting harder and faster.

Wade loved hearing her chant his name.

She pulled his face to hers and slammed her lips onto his. The kiss was feral and wild. His arousal for her grew, sending him into a frenzy. This kiss, he allowed her to dominate. Her tongue pushed forth inside his mouth, sweeping in to taunt his.

His orgasm was racing to him, and Wade refused to come without her. Lifting herself higher, she released a cry.

"Oh, God!" Joy screamed out. Her body shook as she reached her climax. Her eyes were clenched shut, her skin flushed.

It was the most magnificent sight Wade had ever witnessed.

He continued to pound himself into her, crying out while her muscles clamped down on him. He gripped her tight, finally able to let go.

He shouted, his release spilling from him when he paused and buried himself in her fully.

They held each other. Wade refused to move. He

was right where he was supposed to be at the moment, and didn't want to ever leave.

———

Joy let loose a sigh and basked in the afterglow of the most mind-blowing sex she'd ever had. Wade Brooks just kept surprising her, and she didn't know what to expect from him.

They had finally made it over to the couch and crashed on it. He had dragged a soft blanket over them. Her skin practically tingled from their explosive lovemaking.

The television somehow got turned on, but neither of them were paying attention to it. Wade's living room fit him. The last time she had been at his house, she'd only seen a couple of rooms.

The living room was surprisingly spacious, with large windows lining the walls. In the daytime, she was sure it would be bright and airy. The reclaimed wood panels on the ceiling were the highlight, along with the enormous fireplace. It would be cozy in the wintertime, with a huge fire roaring while she and Wade snuggled on the couch.

Her eyes widened upon realizing she was already making plans for the future.

Joy blew out a deep breath and played with the hairs on his chest.

"What's wrong?" Wade's voice rumbled beneath her ears.

She hesitated, unsure if she should be honest.

Never had she been one to hold back her feelings, so she decided to just go ahead and share what was on her mind.

"I've just been thinking that I don't know what to make of us. Do we tell our families and friends? Is this thing between us a secret?" She lifted her head and stared into Wade's eyes. They may have come to a truce, but their families certainly hadn't. Junior's comments at dinner came to mind, and she winced.

"What do you want us to be? I do need to know." His voice lightened as a smile played on his lips. "You can't just use my body any way you want."

Joy burst out laughing. She buried her head against his chest. He pulled her into the crook of his arm.

"I'm being serious," she muttered.

Wade sifted his fingers through her hair, and his smile disappeared.

"We aren't our parents, or our grandparents. There are things they could learn from us. Everything solved by breaking bread together and talking." He entwined their fingers.

"Let's see where this goes, taking it a day at a time.

My father is as stubborn as yours," she murmured. How she was going to break the news to her father that she was sleeping with a Brooks was still a mystery. "You know what my father wants."

She paused, unsure if she should have shared that.

"I know." He sighed, running a hand over his face. "But there is nothing I can do. My father is still in charge of everything on the ranch, and I know he won't sell."

Joy nodded and snagged her lip with her teeth.

"But let's not talk about our fathers," Wade suggested. "What do you say? You and me?" he asked softly.

"Yes," she whispered without hesitation.

Wade grinned and leaned down, pressing a kiss to her mouth. Joy's lips parted immediately to grant his tongue entrance.

Joy moaned and pushed her naked form to Wade's. Her breasts were crushed against his firm chest.

Wade's hand disappeared underneath the blanket and cupped her bottom. He pulled back from her, his smile gentle. "I can think of an activity to take our minds off land agreements and such."

The teasing glint in his eyes had Joy grinning along with him.

"I can too." Joy pushed the Whitaker-Brooks strife to the back of her mind.

Wade's hard length brushed against her.

"What are you thinking?" he asked. His eyebrows rose high.

She moved the cover away and winked at him. She smoothed her hand across his chiseled abdomen and captured his manhood.

"I know something that we will both enjoy and occupy our time." She stroked his long length.

Wade's eyes fluttered closed for a moment before they reopened. He licked his lips and reached for her.

"What is that?" He guided her face to his and took her lips in a bruising kiss. His cock swelled in her hand, and he grasped her closer to him. She continued running hers up the smooth shaft.

Joy broke the kiss. Her breaths were coming hard, but then again, Wade's kisses always left her that way. With a wink, she pushed off the couch and knelt down to where she was at eye level with his magnificent cock. It was a beautiful one. Wide, lengthy, and perfectly shaped.

She glanced up and found Wade staring at her intently. Not breaking the stare, she licked the mushroom tip, tasting his saltiness.

A moan slipped from her.

Wade's chest was rising and falling rapidly.

"Jesus," he whispered.

She guided the tip into her mouth, sealing her lips

around him. A groan sliced through the air. This time, it was Wade's. Joy's heart beat erratically with the thought of bringing him as much pleasure as he had given her.

She introduced as much as she could into her mouth and slid her hand along him, setting a steady rhythm.

A tremor rippled through Wade. Joy's eyes fluttered closed, and she concentrated on her current task.

She wanted to please him. To worship his shaft that had given her so much pleasure.

Wade threaded his fingers through her hair, gently guiding her. His hips moved, thrusting his length deeper into her mouth.

His groans filled the air, and his movements quickened.

"I'm not ready to come yet," Wade gasped. He tugged on her hair, pulling her off of him.

She released his cock with a pout. "But I wasn't done."

He took her by her arm and tugged her up and over him to where her legs straddled him.

"For now, you are." He lined up the tip of his cock to her opening. Wade's fingers dug into her hips, and he drew her down on him.

He impaled her with his long rod, and she released a moan.

"You feel so good inside me," she whimpered. Joy rocked her hips, loving the sensation of the fullness she got from Wade being buried inside her.

She leaned down, pressing a kiss to his lips. Wade wrapped an arm around her and thrust his hips up, sending him deeper.

Joy cried out, but it was captured by Wade's mouth. He continued kissing her while she rode him. Her hands rested on the arm of the couch.

Her hips moved on their own. Joy panted, her body growing sensitive to the sensations coursing through it.

Wade took control of their lovemaking, guiding her up and down his length. He shifted positions by sitting higher, sending him deeper.

Joy's moans grew louder. He consumed her completely.

She pulled up before sinking back down on Wade. The flames of her desire were growing.

She needed more.

Wade pumped harder, his growls echoing around them.

They were both panting, their bodies slick with sweat.

"You're so fucking sexy," Wade growled. "Ride me, cowgirl."

He slipped a hand down between them, and she stiffened when his thumb met her clit.

"Wade," she chanted while digging her nails into the furniture, trying to contain herself. She teetered on the edge of her orgasm, no longer able to keep it at bay.

Wade pressed against her little bud, and she detonated. "Aaahh!"

Her body grew tense, and she rode the ripples of her climax.

Wade stiffened beneath her. His roar tore through the air. Joy continued to rock against him, wrapping her arms around his neck when he exploded.

His warm release filled her.

Joy collapsed on top of Wade, spent.

A small smile played on her lips.

Wade's large hand rested on her back. They both lay together, their breathing erratic.

Joy closed her eyes and relaxed on him. At the moment, she didn't want to think of anything else but them.

Right now, it was him and her, and that's all that truly mattered.

Wade glanced down at his watch, and his heart skipped a beat. It had been an entire two weeks since he had run into Joy and her family at the Notorious C.O.W.

Two glorious weeks of seeing Joy practically every day.

Wade enjoyed her company. He would even go as far as to say that they were officially dating. It had been years since he had actually had someone he considered his girlfriend.

He loved everything about Joy.

Their personalities were similar. She made him laugh, and was extremely competitive about everything.

Most days, she came over in the afternoon after work. It was the highlight of his day.

She should be arriving at any moment.

He had just readied two horses for them. Today he

had a special date planned. He'd gotten the idea a few days ago when she had shared with him how she'd had to scare off some coyotes from their sheep. This was a common occurrence for ranchers.

He, of course, made the wrong comment about her not knowing how to shoot.

He knew he was in trouble the moment her eyes narrowed on him.

"Any day you want to compete, you let me know, Wade Brooks."

Her voice echoed in his head.

Well, today, Joy Whitaker was going to have to put her money where her mouth was.

"Two horses," Carson grunted.

Wade glanced over and saw him and Parker walking into the barn.

He shook his head, knowing his brothers were probably about to bust his balls.

"Were you invited to go for a ride?" Parker asked Carson.

"Me?" Carson snickered. "Hell naw. I don't think we're cool enough to hang out with ol' Wade anymore."

Parker wrapped an arm around the youngest Brooks' shoulder as they strode toward him.

"Don't feel bad, Carson. One day, when you grow up and find a woman, you won't want to hang out with your brothers either," Parker announced. It was good to see Parker in a playful mood. He had been through so much recently, and it was nice to have the old Parker breaking through.

"Y'all are idiots," Wade muttered. He shook his head and returned to his task.

He packed the last of the paper targets in a saddlebag and turned to his brothers. The spot he had planned to take her to was already together. He had stopped by earlier to set up old tin cans and glasses at the range they used.

"Is that what it is?" Carson gasped, holding his chest in shock. "Well, shit. What about the bunnies I hung out with last weekend? They don't count?"

"You need to leave those women alone. They only want one thing." Wade jokingly shoved Carson.

Carson put up his fist, playfully throwing it. Wade immediately blocked it, not above tussling with him.

It had been a while since they'd engaged in a friendly fight.

Carson grinned. "Hell, that's all I'm looking for."

They circled each other, with Parker observing. He adjusted his hat and folded his arms.

"I'd have to say today, my money would be on Wade," Parker snickered.

"Why? 'Cause he don't want to get his clothes dirty for his little date with Joy?" Carson responded. Moving quick, he rushed Wade, and caught him by the waist.

Carson's speed and strength had come in handy during his college football days.

"Always got jokes," Wade snorted, landing a quick left to Carson's side.

Carson released him and stepped back.

Their breaths were labored from their rough-housing.

"Don't worry. I'm not going to get you dirty, bro," Carson chuckled. He straightened and held his side with a slight wince. "We wouldn't want you to not be presentable for your date."

Wade shook his head and smiled. He wrapped his arm around Carson's neck. Knocking his baseball cap off, he ruffled his hair as he and Parker had done when they were kids.

"Don't worry about my date," he said.

"You and Joy have been spending a lot of time together. What's up?" Parker asked, his gaze connecting with Wade's.

He released Carson and shrugged, fixing his shirt.

"She's been spending the night too," Carson snickered. He dipped down and snagged his hat from the ground and dusted it off. "A lot."

Wade's gaze cut to Carson, who wagged his eyebrows at him. Carson was nosy as hell. How the hell did he know that?

Laughing, Wade swept a hand through his hair. It

looked like he was busted. He was close to his siblings, and felt comfortable talking about Joy with them. He wouldn't be going into intimate details or anything, though. There were some things that should be kept private, even between brothers.

"Joy and I are together," Wade admitted. It felt good to get it off his chest and say it out loud. He had to keep a goofy grin from spreading. "I really like her. She's an amazing woman."

Images of her spread out on his bed came to mind, and he swallowed hard.

His cock twitched.

He had to push those memories away. There would be no way Parker and Carson would let him live down an erection in the barn.

"Does Pa know you're dating a Whitaker?" Parker asked softly.

Wade shook his head. He hadn't wanted to share that information with his father just yet. Jonah usually came out of the house early in the mornings. They would take him along the ranch in one of the four wheelers. The old man enjoyed the outings. It wasn't on his horse, but he didn't fuss anymore.

At least not about driving around in the carts.

Jonah Brooks always found something to complain about.

But the fresh air and small tasks out on the ranch

were doing him some good. His coloring was looking better, and even the physical therapist agreed getting him out on the land and moving around was helping.

By the afternoon, he was back in the house with Eliana fussing and driving her crazy.

Joy had yet to tell her father. She'd shared with Wade that her mother, Georgy, and her sister, Lexi, knew of them. She wasn't brave enough to tell her father yet, even though she understood she had to.

Wade realized this wasn't right, and soon they would have to tell their fathers. He just wanted to ensure his was strong enough to know he was dating Whitaker's daughter. It was a weak excuse, he knew, but seeing his father collapsing on the ground wasn't something that just disappeared from his mind.

Wade could still see the color drain from his face before he had hit the ground.

He blinked, trying to clear the memory.

He and Joy were too old to be running around in secret.

They would have to tell their fathers, even if they did it together.

"Hey, fellas. Look who I found," Maddy called out from the doorway.

They turned around to find Maddy and Joy standing next to each other. They both giggled, glancing at each other.

Wade's heart skipped a beat.

Joy was dressed in cutoff shorts and a plaid shirt tied at the waist. Her dark hair was contained in two braids on either side of her head.

He swallowed hard, trying to guess what she had on underneath the clothes.

His girl loved lingerie, and he loved peeling it off of her. It was like getting to unwrap his Christmas gifts early.

He had eyes only for Joy as she walked toward him.

"Hey, Maddy. Hey, Joy." Carson nodded to them.

"Hey, Carson," the girls echoed simultaneously.

Maddy went to Parker, who pulled her in for a hug and kissed her forehead.

"How's my Maddy girl?" Parker asked, his hand resting on her small baby bump.

"Better now." Maddy grinned and looked up to Parker.

"Hey, there," Joy greeted, smiling.

Wade opened his arms for her. She walked straight into them and wrapped her arms around his waist. Her body felt so damn good against his. It had been too long since he had seen her.

Last night, she had not stayed over, but had gone home, citing she had to get an early start today.

"I missed you," he murmured, leaning down and pressing a kiss to her lips.

The barn had grown silent. He and Joy turned to find Maddy, Parker, and Carson with shit-eating grins on their faces.

He had forgotten they were there the second his gaze had met Joy's.

Joy ran a hand across her face.

"Do I have something on my face?" she asked.

Wade smiled, knowing he had officially just claimed her in front of them, which he was fine with. He never hid anything from his brothers, and wasn't going to start now.

"Why are y'all grinning like that? What's wrong with you?"

Wade chuckled and rested his chin on her head. "Before you came in here, Parker and Carson were giving me the third degree about us," he admitted.

"We were not," Carson sputtered. "We were just inquiring about your intentions with our dear brother."

Wade rolled his eyes. Joy released a giggle and glanced up at him. She patted him on his abdomen and turned back to them.

"Don't worry, fellas. Your brother's virtue has been—"

"Long gone," Parker interjected, sending them all into a fit of laughter.

"Be that as it may, I'm finding your brother very useful," Joy replied haughtily.

Wade pinched Joy on her ass. Squealing, she tried to squirm away from him.

"I'm just useful?" he growled playfully.

Maddy covered her face as she burst out laughing. Tears streamed down her cheeks while she fanned herself.

"It's about time there's another woman around you guys. I need something to break up all the testosterone," she said.

"We're not that bad," Parker scoffed. He pulled Maddy in front of him and wrapped an arm around her. He turned his attention to Wade. "Where are you two going?"

"It was going to be a surprise, but I might as well tell her now." Wade slid his hand down and entwined his fingers with Joy's. "A certain woman, who will not be named, has issued a challenge. She apparently thinks she's a better shot than me, so we are headed out to settle this."

"Are you serious?" Joy spun to him, her grin wide. There was her famous competitive glint in her eyes. "Are you sure you want to tell them that we're competing? I wouldn't want your little pride to be hurt in front of your brothers." She poked him in the chest.

"First of all, there's nothing small about my pride," he joked, drawing her close to him.

She gasped, and tried to push him away. He hoped

175

she wasn't embarrassed by his innuendo, but they were only around his brothers and Maddy. They'd heard worse.

"And second, you won't be winning today. I guarantee that."

His brothers snickered.

"A date with a woman and guns, now that is what I'm talking about." Carson gave them all a salute and strolled toward the entrance of the barn. He spun around and walked backward. "I'm going to have to find me one."

"What? A gun?" Maddy called out after him.

"Nope. A woman!" He grinned and turned, disappearing out of sight.

"Your brother is a nut." Parker shook his head. His hand dropped back down to Maddy's stomach. "Let's go, babe. I'm sure we have to round Tyler up."

They ambled toward the back entrance of the barn.

"You may have better success than me. Maybe we should get some rope and wrangle him like y'all do the cows," Maddy suggested.

Wade was so happy for Parker and Maddy. They were in love, and it showed the minute they were next to each other. Maddy was good for his brother, and Wade loved her like a sister.

Joy laughed and turned to Wade. "Tyler sounds like me when I was a kid."

"That nephew of mine loves the outdoors, and will try to hide from his parents when it's time to go home." Wade tugged her along and headed out of the barn where the horses were waiting for them. He snagged the saddlebag he had prepared and hefted it onto his shoulder. "I hope you're ready for today's ass kicking."

Joy wagged a finger at him. "Don't start talking your shit, Brooks."

He grinned and pulled her close, dropping a hard kiss to her lips. He loved seeing her riled up.

She just didn't know how good of a shot he was.

He was going to have to burst her little bubble and show her his skills.

"You're looking mighty good on that horse, girl," Wade teased.

Joy glanced over her shoulder and grinned.

"What're you doing looking?" she joked. Her cheeks hurt from smiling so much. The second they'd left on horseback, they had been flirting back and forth. She sat up straighter in the saddle.

Joy had been in a playful mood when she got dressed. She felt like being a total country bumpkin. Short-shorts, her shirt tied at her waist, and she'd put her hair into two thick French braids.

Can't get any more country than this.

Wade's eyes lifted to hers, and his grin widened.

"I'm liking the way you're sitting in that saddle," he admitted.

"Is that so?" She batted her eyelashes as he brought his horse to ride alongside hers. Had she known they were going riding, she would have brought Jazzy.

Dixie, the mare they'd lent her, was an intelligent, friendly horse who'd immediately taken to Joy.

Her gaze landed on Wade, and she would have to admit, he was mighty fine. He wore a soft T-shirt with his jeans and boots, and today, had on a Stetson. He was the epitome of sexy cowboy.

"You're not looking too bad over there, Brooks." She tossed him a wink.

His smile widened, and he lifted his hat and tipped it to her.

"Glad you think so," he replied.

They fell into a fit of laughter. She was excited about the date he had planned. It just showed he was as competitive as she was. She had issued the challenge, not knowing he was going to make them go through with it.

If he wanted to get his behind whooped by a girl today, then she was just the one to do it.

"Follow me. We're almost there," Wade announced. He trotted ahead of her and Dixie, leading the way.

"Come on, girl." Joy kicked her heels in to speed up the mare. She followed Wade through a wooded area for a few minutes. The path narrowed, and Dixie was extremely well-trained. She walked behind Wade and his horse without even needing to be instructed to do so. Soon, they came out to an opening that revealed beautiful rolling hills off in the distance.

Up ahead of them were man-made target posts. Cans and large glass jars were set up already.

"Someone came out here and got it organized?" she asked, impressed. Her heart skipped at the thought of him coming out earlier to prepare for their date. She glanced around and saw they had everything they would need.

He pulled his horse to a halt and turned to her. "I wanted to make sure there was no reason you would try to back out." He dismounted and walked toward her.

"Wild horses couldn't drag me away from this," she chuckled.

He stopped by Dixie and held out his hand for her. She normally would have fussed and proclaimed that she didn't need a man helping her from a horse, but she kept silent. Wade was being the sweetheart he was.

"Thank you, sir. Aren't you a gentleman."

He grinned. "Darlin', you just don't know."

Taking his hand, she threw her leg over Dixie and allowed him to help her off. She purposely slid her body down his, allowing every inch of their bodies to meet.

Once on the ground, she wrapped her arms around

his neck and brought his head close to hers for a proper kiss.

Joy wasn't above using her feminine wiles to rattle Wade.

He tore his lips from hers and grinned.

"Don't think I don't know what you're up to, pretty lady," Wade murmured. He pressed his lips to hers for a chaste kiss and drew her closer.

She bit back a whimper at the feeling of his erection straining against her stomach.

"What are you talking about?" Joy called on her dusty acting skills to try to play innocent.

Wade ran his hands over her ass and gave it a squeeze. The feel of his hardness had her knees growing weak.

Maybe this wasn't a good idea.

Another kiss, and he backed away from her.

"It's not going to work. I'm going to win." He laughed and walked back over to his horse. He took the saddlebag and threw it over his shoulder.

"Hey," she scoffed, following behind him.

She was impressed by his setup, and could tell it was an area they had used many times. He took a few things from his bag and set them down on a wooden table that was constructed near a tree. Yeah, Wade and his brothers came here often. Their range was thoughtfully built, and had everything they would need.

Resting her hands on her hips, she turned to him. "You know you have an unfair advantage."

"Just because my brothers and I come out here at least once a month, you think I have an advantage?" That sexy grin of his was in place. He marched over to her and gently slid a pair of protective glasses over her eyes.

Her body was going haywire.

She was always aroused when she was around him.

How the hell was she going to concentrate on shooting a gun with him watching her? She'd be lucky if she could get a gun to fire with him standing so close to her.

Wade leaned down and kissed her.

"Right now, I just need to make sure those pretty brown eyes of yours are protected," he murmured before capturing her lips again.

Joy melted against him when the kiss deepened.

Wade tore his lips from hers, both of them breathing hard. He stared into her eyes. His rigid erection teased her, and she was sure her panties were drenched.

Wade had a way of doing that to her.

He pressed his lips to hers again, then walked away. His muttering echoed through the air. Joy's heart was racing. She couldn't believe how quick her body had gone up in flames the second he'd touched her.

She fanned herself as she watched Wade pull two rifles from twin leather holster cases from his horse.

She couldn't take her eyes off him as he returned to her. He held out the rifles for her to pick from.

He winked at her. "Ladies first."

She eyed the two rifles he offered. She folded her arms and raised an eyebrow at him.

"Really?" she asked.

"What?" he asked, confused.

"You brought a .308 and a .22. Who really is supposed to shoot at this distance with a .22?"

He blinked at her. A sheepish expression came over his face.

"I didn't know—"

"Didn't know what?" She laid it on thick. He apparently didn't think she would be able to handle the bigger caliber weapon. Everyone knew that a .22 was for beginners, or even children. What was he thinking?

Men.

Oh, was she going to teach him.

"I figured you may need something small..." His words trailed off. He blew out a deep breath and handed her the .308.

"Look at this beauty," she gasped, snatching it from him. She immediately ensured the chambers were empty. "A Ruger Precision. It's beautiful. I've been wanting to get my hands on one of these babies."

Wade's eyebrows jumped up. "Why am I even surprised?"

"What country girl doesn't know how to handle a rifle, Wade Brooks?" She shook her head and walked toward the table so she could assess the weapon. It was heavier than she thought it would be. She'd actually looked at it online a few months ago, but hadn't had a chance to go check it out at the store. From what she'd heard, it was excellent for long-distance shooting.

After she'd done her checks on it, she held it up and peered through the scope, aiming the weapon at one of the targets.

She tried as best as she could to ignore how close Wade was standing next to her.

"Everything good?" he asked.

"Appears to be. How many rounds did you bring?"

"Enough," he replied. He placed a couple of magazines down on the table, along with a few boxes of ammo. "Are you ready, pretty lady?"

"Oh, don't you worry yourself, Wade Brooks. I'll be real gentle with you," she teased. She snatched up the magazine and inserted it into the rifle.

The sound of hooves gained their attention. Joy turned to find three of the ranch hands headed their way. The men pulled up on their horses.

"What's up fellas?" Wade walked over to them.

They all echoed a greeting and nodded to her.

She'd known Stan and Rashad, who were employed at Blazing Eagle, for a long time. The other hand, Mike, had worked for her family a few seasons ago. He had only stayed with them for a year before he up and quit.

"We were just checking on the herd and figured we'd give Mike a full tour while we were out," Stan replied.

"So, what're y'all about to do out here?" Rashad asked.

He dismounted and adjusted his cap. He was a nice-looking man, and Joy had heard he and Yani Polk were now an item.

Yani was a popular hair stylist in town who Joy was friends with and used her services. Seeing Rashad reminded her that she needed to make an appointment with Yani for a haircut.

"Well, Joy thinks she can outshoot me. So, we are here to settle the score," Wade announced.

Stan and Mike also hopped down from their horses and walked over to Wade.

Stan, Rashad, and Mike laughed while glancing at her. She rolled her eyes.

"Really? You're not going to let her show you up, are you?" Stan chortled.

"Hey, I'm right here," she said, laughing.

"Sorry, Joy. He pays me," Stan replied with a sheepish look.

Joy observed how the men were around Wade. They were respectful with him, even if teasing him about him setting up the shootout.

"Well, I don't know about you fellas, but I'm staying to watch," Rashad stated.

Wade glanced at her and winked.

"We now have an audience to watch us, darling. We wouldn't want you telling a fib on how bad I beat ya."

Joy narrowed her eyes on him.

It was on.

"It's your pride on the line. They are witnesses to a girl who can shoot better than you."

"Well, then, Whitaker. Let the games begin," Wade said.

She stuck out her tongue and walked over to the shooting post. She snatched the earplugs from the table and inserted them to protect her hearing.

She would need to whip them back out later to make sure she was able to hear Wade's groveling after she whipped his butt.

He stood a few feet from her to give her some room. Everyone grew silent as she aimed the weapon and focused through the scope. The rifle was smooth and sleek, fitting in her hands perfectly. She aimed it true, focusing in on the first glass jar.

Safety off.

Using all the tricks her father had taught her, she relaxed. The targets were two hundred yards away, and she was confident in hitting the mark.

The large mason jar was in her sights.

Her finger rested on the trigger.

The wind blew slightly. She factored that into her calculations, ignoring Wade and the others.

She pulled back on the trigger.

Bang.

The shot rang out with a solid recoil.

The bullet whizzed through the air and shattered the glass. Shifting her focus, she moved to the next target, hitting that one. Within seconds, she'd cleared all of them.

Didn't miss one.

She lowered the weapon and glanced over at Wade.

Clapping echoed around her.

"Not bad, Whitaker," Wade murmured. His lips were curled up into a slight grin. "That's some damn good shooting. Where did you learn to shoot like that?"

Joy rested a hand on her hip with her head held proud.

"My father." Davis Whitaker, Sr. believed all his children should learn to defend their land and animals. There were plenty of summers where he had her and her siblings out target practicing. It was important they could hit the target, since coyotes and other animals were always trying to sneak and steal a lamb or two.

"One of you mind helping out with the targets?" Wade called out over his shoulder.

"Got it," Rashad responded.

Wade ambled over to her and held his hand out for the weapon. She held on to it tighter, keeping it pointed at the ground.

"What? You don't want to use the .22?" she asked haughtily.

Grinning, he glanced over at the table where the other rifle sat. He turned his attention back to her and laughed.

"Not today."

"Next time—"

"I know to bring two big guns," he finished, smirking.

Joy grinned and handed him the weapon. His fingers brushed hers, and he grabbed her by the waist. He landed a kiss on her lips before moving her.

She backed away. Rashad had finished replacing the targets with other odd items. He ran to a safe distance with the other hands.

The competition was officially on.

Joy couldn't take her eyes off Wade and how he handled the rifle. It was like second nature to him. The ease and comfort he displayed while holding it was downright sexy.

"All right, boss. Don't let me down," Stan called out. Chuckles went up all around. "I got lunch riding on this."

Joy grinned and peeked over at them. Rashad lifted his hat to her.

He had her back.

She laughed.

He better had, or she'd have to have a little conversation with Yani about it.

"Don't worry, Stan. You'll be eating a good meal soon," Wade announced.

Joy snorted.

The air grew silent until the shots thundered.

Joy glanced over at the targets and saw he'd hit every single one of them. The competition grew fierce.

If was clearly a female versus male game, but Joy didn't mind. She could hang with the best of them.

The shootout ended in a damn tie.

Neither of them missed.

The competitive nature in her wasn't satisfied.

She wanted to win.

"Well, guess no one will be buying lunches," Mike guffawed.

The hands walked back over to their horses.

"Oh, there's plenty for us to wager against." Stan laughed, slapping Mike on the back.

Stan, Rashad, and Mike mounted their horses and left.

Joy observed Wade gather the weapons and left-over rounds.

She pouted, watching him stride over to their grazing horses, returning the weapons to their sheaths.

Turning around, she moved over to the edge of the landing and stared out onto the land. It was beautiful. And even though there was no declared winner, she had enjoyed herself.

She walked a few more feet, basking in the feel of the thick grass beneath her. Caught up in the splendor of the land, she didn't hear Wade come up behind her until his warm arms wrapped around her, bringing her back against him. He pressed close to her and nibbled on her ear.

"Your competitive nature is so damn sexy," Wade murmured.

"Really?" She held on to his arm and enjoyed the feeling being enveloped in his arms. Her head rolled to the side to allow him to nuzzle the crook of her neck.

He pressed kisses to her skin while his hand caressed her bare stomach.

"Yes," he hissed. He nipped her with his teeth, and she jumped slightly. "And this outfit, I absolutely approve of." His warm breath blew over her skin, sending chills down her spine.

Joy reached up and threaded her fingers through his thick hair.

Wade's hand slipped underneath her shirt and shoved her bra out of the way, freeing her breasts.

A moan slipped from her as he cupped her mound.

"I thought of you when I put it on," she teased.

He massaged her while his other hand slid south. He flicked open the button to her shorts and pushed his way inside.

His finger parted her folds and connected with her clit.

Jesus, the man never needs instructions.

"You are just so thoughtful." He strummed her swollen nub.

Joy spread her legs, allowing him to have full access to her.

Her breath caught in her throat. She tightened her grip on his hair, needing to hold on to something.

"Wade," she moaned.

"You know I love hearing you say my name," he growled. He nipped her again with his teeth, soothing her skin with his tongue.

Joy could barely concentrate. She didn't care they were out in the open. Both she and Wade loved the outdoors, so it didn't matter to her that he was close to bringing her to orgasm on his finger where God and whoever just so happened to come by could see them.

His movements grew faster. Her hips rotated as she rode his hand.

"Wade," she repeated breathlessly. It was the only word she could think of.

There was no doubt this man was consuming her every thought. The pleasure he wrung out of her kept him on her mind. He knew his way around her body and how to get a rise out of her.

"I love how your body fucking responds to me," he whispered.

She whimpered, thrusting her chest out farther. His grip tightened on her breasts while he cupped and caressed her. He pinched her nipple, and she cried out. "Dammit, Joy, you're so damn wet."

Tremors swarmed through her.

She was writhing in his arms, unable to stand still any longer. Her knees grew weak. She was teetering on the edge of her release.

"Oh," she gasped.

He applied the sweetest pressure to her clit, sending her skyrocketing to the stars. Her climax hit her hard. Her cry echoed through the air, and she coasted along the waves of her orgasm.

Wade gripped her tight when her knees buckled.

Joy closed her eyes, leaning back against his warm,

solid frame. Drawing in strength she didn't know she possessed, she stood upright and turned.

She didn't care what she looked like with her shorts open and her shirt and bra skewed.

Wade drew her back to him and leaned down, crushing his lips to hers. Within seconds, their clothes were on the ground, and Joy found herself on top of them with Wade braced above her.

One thrust, and he was buried deep inside of her.

"Fuck. You're so wet," he gasped.

He held himself still. The muscles in his neck were strained. Joy brought his head down to hers and kissed him. It was deep and passionate. Wade pulled back and brushed a few wayward strands of hair from her face, staring into her eyes.

"This may be a little rough, baby."

Joy smiled.

She locked her ankles behind him.

"Bring it on, Brooks."

"It's okay, Sara. Dr. Hutson will be here soon enough," Wade muttered. He stood beside Stan and Mike, staring at the cow, moaning in distress. Her eyes were wide. She wasn't doing too well.

They were waiting for the veterinarian to arrive. Wade and the hands had tried everything they could think of to help Sara. She was one of the beloved cows they'd had for years. She had just recently had a calf during the last breeding season.

"This can't be right," Mike said. He crossed his arms and eyed her.

"I've never seen her act this way," Stan mumbled.

Sara pressed against the gate and let loose another cry.

Wade shook his head. "Me neither."

It was a hot day, and he was sweating and frustrated. At least she hadn't gotten down on the ground. She was strong, and a fighter. Whatever this was, he hoped it was something the good doctor could take care of.

His phone vibrated in his pocket. He pulled it out and saw a text from Dr. Hutson.

I'll be there in less than fifteen.

Wade sent off a reply with their location.

"Let's move her away from the other cows." Wade motioned over to the other side of the railing where she wouldn't be near the others. Her calf stood by, trying to get to her.

Mike and Stan struggled to get her to move.

Wade found some rope where he could tie her to the metal fence where the doctor wouldn't have to chase her.

Once they had her situated, the calf started crying and hitting the fence to get to his momma.

"Should we let him in?" Mike asked.

"Nah, he'll be okay. At least he can still see her." Wade took his hat off and pushed his fingers through his damp hair. They couldn't afford to have anything happen to Sara. She was a prized breeder. "Doc should be here any minute. We can chill until he gets here."

Mike sat on a tree stump that was located right near the gated corral attached to the smaller barn they had for housing some of the cattle.

Stan and Wade leaned back against the fence.

"So, you and Joy, huh?" Stan chuckled, glancing

over at Wade. "She's a real sweet girl. Y'all look good together."

Wade grinned. "Yeah, she is."

Stan had worked for the ranch for years, and was someone he trusted. He considered him a friend. The hand was newly single, and had been out with Wade and his brothers a few times. They had taken him out to celebrate his divorce a year ago.

"She's good for me."

Just thinking of Joy put a shit-eating grin on his face. He didn't need anyone to tell him; he could feel it. Things between them were moving fast, but Wade was okay with that. She was sexy, smart, headstrong, and kept him on his toes.

Everything about her took his breath away any time he was in her presence. He'd never responded to another woman like this before.

It had him thinking of a future with her.

He didn't want to be away from her.

Even for a day.

"You just need to watch her," Mike declared.

Wade's smile disappeared. He tensed and glared at the hand. He didn't know Mike too well. Parker had hired him, thinking he would be a good fit for Blazing Eagle.

"What the hell is that supposed to mean?" Wade

clenched his fists. Who the hell was this guy to speak ill of Joy?

Mike apparently saw the change in Wade. He held up his hands.

"I'm just saying. I used to work on her family's ranch. I know what kind of people they are." Mike gave a dry laugh.

Wade narrowed his eyes on Mike. He pushed his hat back so he could meet the gaze of the hand.

"Type of people?" he questioned.

What. The. Fuck.

He prayed Mike wasn't going to go on a racist tangent. Wade didn't tolerate people who disliked others for the color of their skin. There was enough hate in the world, and he'd be damned if that made its way onto his family's land.

"I think you need to explain yourself." He took a step toward Mike, but Stan jumped in between them and pushed Wade back.

"Whoa, now. I'm sure Mike didn't mean anything by it. Did you?" Stan turned to Mike, all the while keeping his body between him and Wade.

Wade was fuming. He would defend Joy without a second thought. No one would speak ill of his woman in his presence. Joy was a good person with a big heart.

"Look, I like it around here. The job is good, hours are great, and the pay is amazing. I wouldn't jeopardize this. I used to work for her father, and believe me when I say that Davis Whitaker hates anything to do with the Blazing Eagle Ranch." Mike took a step back and shook his head. He wiped a hand over his face and turned his attention back to Stan and Wade. "I can't tell you how many times he'd rant and rave about the Brooks family and how y'all are land thieves who break deals. I don't know what he was talking about. What is this? The eighteen hundreds? It's like he wanted to brainwash anyone who worked at the Fox Run."

Stan glanced over his shoulder at Wade.

"Joy is not her father," Wade growled. He moved toward Mike, but Stan shoved him back.

"Forget I said anything. I'm not trying to lose a good job over this. I was even hoping to stay on and become full-time. I've heard things, and wasn't going to say anything, but then she started coming around."

Wade tried to push Stan out of the way, but the guy was solid muscle.

"Get him out of here," Wade snapped. He was not one to listen to gossip.

"Maybe you should hear him out. If there is talk amongst the hands, we can put a stop to it." Stan met Wade's glare head-on. "Calm down, Wade. Listen to him."

Wade shook Stan's hands off and took a step back. His breaths were coming fast, and he was strung tight.

If there was gossip amongst the hands about Joy, then he was going to personally put an end to it.

"Talk."

Mike's eyes were wide as he pulled his hat off. He wiped his forehead with the back of his arm as he visibly swallowed hard before replacing his hat.

"There ain't much." He nervously glanced at Wade. "I have a few buddies who still work over at Fox Run, and they said that Davis is willing to do whatever he needs to to get his land back."

Wade refused to believe Joy would do something as to what Mike was implying. He walked a few feet away and swiped a hand across his face. He grimaced at the rough bristles on his skin. He hadn't shaved that morning.

Wade turned back to Mike and waved a hand. "Just go."

"I'm not fired, am I?" Mike asked, worried.

Wade couldn't fire him over sharing gossip. From what he had seen from the short time he'd been working for them, he was dependable, a hard worker, and appeared to be a good man. Parker had a sixth sense about people, and wouldn't have hired him on if he didn't think Mike wasn't a good fit for the ranch.

"Stan and I can handle Sara. Go radio in to Carson and see what he needs help with." Wade knew his younger brother was installing a cattle sweep and a few bale feeders for the cattle, and every extra hand would help get them up and working faster.

"Yes, sir. I truly didn't mean anything." Mike spun on his heels and jogged over to one of the ATVs parked nearby.

Now doubts were creeping into his head as he watched Mike drive away. He tried to push them down, but he couldn't.

The Whitakers had been after his father to sign back over their land. The deal dated back years, and Wade had never taken an interest in it before. If Jonah didn't want to sell it back to them, then Hell would have to freeze over before he changed his mind.

Wade and his brothers didn't have any say so over the land until it was turned over to them. Jonah had the controlling hand over the ranch.

Joy wouldn't stoop so low as to try to get close to him to get her family land back.

Would she?

Wade shook those thoughts from his head. He knew Joy. She was many things, but a deceitful liar was not one of them.

Mike didn't really know Wade like that, so why would he lie?

Who else was talking about Joy and their relationship?

He would have to get to the bottom of this.

"You going to be all right?" Stan's voice broke through Wade's thoughts.

"Yeah." Wade glanced back over at Sara, having forgotten about her for a brief moment. The poor cow was in pain. He could see it plain as day by her posture, and she wasn't fighting being tied against the railings. Her breathing was becoming labored.

Something was definitely wrong.

Tires flying along the gravel had Wade and Stan rotating around to see the new arrival. A truck drove up and parked near them.

The doctor was here. He exited his truck and grabbed a few things out of the back seat before walking toward them.

Guy Hutson was a second-generation veterinarian. He was the primary physician for the animals on the farm, along with his father. The elder Hutson was no longer doing farm calls, and had turned it over to Guy.

"How she doing?" Guy asked, coming over to them with a large black bag. He swung his stethoscope around his neck.

"Not sure, Doc. I've never seen her like this," Stan replied.

Wade had to fight to keep his attention on the problem at hand. His anger was finally dispersing. It wouldn't have been good if he'd put his hands on his employee and kicked his ass.

Blowing out a deep breath, he focused on the conversation between Stan and Guy.

"She appears to be in pain," Wade mentioned.

Guy smiled and walked into the corral with Sara.

"Hey, girl. How's it going?" Guy spoke to her in a calm voice.

Sara was skittish, crying out, and tried to pull on the rope to break free.

Guy dropped his bag on the ground and put his stethoscope in his ears to listen to Sara while murmuring quietly to her. She finally calmed down and stood still for the doctor. He knocked on her belly in different areas.

Wade and Stan waited while the doctor assessed the troubled cow.

"Well, don't worry, fellas. She'll be all right." Guy removed his stethoscope from his ears and looked over at them. "It's good that you called me when you did. She's bloated."

"What?" Stan and Wade shared a concerned look.

"She has gas trapped inside of her. It's starting to push against her lungs, making it hard for her to breathe." Guy moved over to his bag and opened it. Pulling out a few items, he returned to Sara. "I just need to release the gas, and then she should be right as rain."

Wade sighed, glad that the doctor could aid her.

"Anything you can do to help her, we would appreciate it," Wade replied.

"This won't take much." Gus grinned. He held up a sharp instrument and began explaining what he would need to do.

Wade trusted the doctor with the care of their animals.

"I'll have to puncture her side with this to create an escape for the gas. I'll give her a shot of antibiotics, and she'll be good by tonight."

Joy drove down the dirt road that led to her family's home. She had an itch to do a little shopping, so she'd ran into town. Her favorite store, Lace and Dreams, a lingerie boutique ran by Mrs. Garret, had received a new shipment. Of course, Mrs. Garret had emailed Joy her current sales, and that was got her there.

She had been unable to resist going in to check out the new items. While in Shady Springs, she'd even browsed some of the other shops, making a nice little afternoon of it.

Joy grinned. She couldn't wait for Wade to see her new, sexy items.

He loved taking her out of her lingerie.

She had to agree with the man. It always looked better on his floor.

Joy arrived at the house and parked her pickup in her normal spot. Her brother's truck was there. He must have stuck around later than normal. Knowing him, he was probably planning to stay for dinner before heading to his place.

Glancing at the porch, she saw her father sitting in his favorite rocker. She killed the engine and got out. The dogs immediately came running for her.

"Can I get my things out the truck first before y'all attack me?" Joy laughed. They yipped and barked, jumping on her. She had to pause and rub each and every one of their heads. "Okay, move."

Joy couldn't help but giggle at them. They always acted as if they hadn't seen her in years whenever she left for a few hours.

They grew even more excited as she pulled her bags out of the truck. She slammed the door shut and turned toward the house. They jumped up, trying to sniff the bags as if looking to see if she had brought them anything.

Normally she did, but this time, she hadn't made a stop at the small pet store.

Her father's shrill whistle cut through the air. The dogs instantly calmed down and whined as they walked alongside her.

"Let her get on the porch," her father ordered.

The dogs instantly backed away, running around the front, chasing after each other.

Her father had a commanding tone that anyone would be stupid to go against. The dogs knew who their true master was.

Joy shook her head and climbed the stairs.

"Hey, Dad." She smiled at her father and blew him a kiss. She had planned to make a beeline into the house so she could put her items away. She didn't really want her father to know that she had shopped at Lace and Dreams.

"Joy, come sit with me." She immediately grew nervous.

Licking her suddenly dry lips, she jerked her head into a nod and walked over to him. She sat on the other rocking chair and placed her bags by her feet where he wouldn't see them.

They rocked together in a strained silence. The dogs had run off somewhere behind the house, their barks echoing off in the distance.

Her stomach was filled with dread. Without asking, she could tell something was wrong.

What? She had no clue.

Finally, her father broke the silence.

"Your mother tells me you're dating a fella," Davis stated.

Joy nodded. "I am."

"I don't understand young folks nowadays. When I courted your mother, I came to the house and introduced myself to her father. There wasn't any running around in secret. We had respect for our elders."

"Daddy," she gasped. "You know I respect you."

Now she felt the lowest of low. She loved her father dearly, and hated seeing him upset.

"Apparently, Wade Brooks doesn't. I'm not surprised, seeing as who his father is." Davis turned his gaze to her, and she sat back in her seat. He was pissed.

"You knew?"

"There are no secretes between your mother and I. She told me as soon as she found out. I waited to see if you would say anything, but it looks like I would have been waiting for the cows to come home."

Tears slid down her face. "I didn't know how to tell you. Blame me. I wasn't sure how you would react," she admitted.

Davis leaned forward and rested his forearms on his knees. He turned his gaze out onto the land before them.

"He's a Brooks, baby. You could date any other fella in this town, and you decided to get in bed with the enemy. The same family who refused to sell our land back."

"It wasn't Wade. He's not his father, and I'm not

you." She wiped the tears from her face. How many times had she heard the story of what the Brooks had done to her family? Not all the Brooks.

Just one.

Jonah.

"All of that happened before either of us were born," she continued.

Her father stood from his chair and dragged a hand over his head. He focused his hardened eyes on her.

"It doesn't matter. You should be loyal to our family name. I've told you repeatedly what they did to our family."

Joy jumped up from her chair and blocked his exit to the front door.

"I am loyal, but it's not fair that I have to choose between people I love." She paused. Her eyes widened, and she stared at her father, unable to believe the words that had just spilled from her lips.

Love Wade?

Did she?

Her father's shoulders slumped, and he stared off in the distance. "Love, eh?"

"I guess I do have feelings for him. He really makes me happy, Daddy. We are so alike, and he's good for me."

Admitting all of this to her father was like a weight

being lifted from her shoulders. Now, all she would have to do was tell Wade how she felt about him.

Her vision blurred as the tears continued to fill her eyes. She didn't know why she was so emotional all of a sudden, but realizing she was in love with Wade was a life-changing moment.

Davis turned back to Joy. Having seen her tears, he cursed and opened his arms. Davis Whitaker, Sr. never could handle his daughters' tears.

"Come here," he murmured.

Joy flew into his arms, where he held her tight. She squeezed her eyes shut, trying not to cry.

"If he didn't treat you well, he'd be having a little chat with my shotgun." Davis pressed a kiss to the top of her head.

"What's going on out here?" her mother asked, coming out of the house.

Junior was right behind her. Joy stepped back from their father and wiped her face.

"Nothing," she mumbled.

"She finally came clean as to who she's been sneaking with," her father admitted, resting a hand on Joy's shoulder.

"Dating?" Junior slid his hands into his pockets, his lips curled up into a grin.

Joy rolled her eyes at him. She was surprised how

calm her father was acting. It was her brother she was worried about.

"Who?" Junior asked.

"A Brooks," her father replied.

"Are you fucking kidding me?" Junior whipped around on her. His eyes narrowed, and his nostrils flared. "Son of a bitch."

Junior tore off down the stairs.

"Junior!" Joy hollered, following behind him. She had a funny feeling he would react this way. Her brother had a short temper, and when it came to the Brookses, it took little to nothing to set him off. "Where the hell are you going?"

"Which one?" He spun around on her suddenly.

She barely missed crashing into him.

"What are you going to do? Go off and fight him because we're seeing each other?" she screamed.

Georgy and Davis yelled for Junior to come back, but he ignored them.

"Which one, Joy? Don't play with me," he snarled. Junior's chest was rising and falling fast. He was beyond pissed. When he got this angry, it was better to get out of his way.

But not this time.

She knew her brother wouldn't raise a hand to her, but Wade was a different story. Junior always felt he had to protect her, but this was one time she wished he would keep his nose out of her life.

"It's none of your business. I don't need you fighting for me over nothing," Joy snapped. If she wanted to have a relationship with Wade, then that was her decision.

"Who?" Junior hollered.

"Wade," her father calmly replied, walking down the stairs.

Joy stared at him, unable to believe he was fanning the flames. She spun around to see Junior hopping into his truck, slamming the door shut. The wheels dug into the gravel as he backed out of his spot.

Joy took off running to her vehicle, her heart racing. Jumping into her truck, she took off behind him.

"Shit!" she screamed.

What the hell was going on?

Her brother had just lost his damn mind. She reached for her phone, but realized it was still on the porch. She couldn't call Wade to warn him.

Hell, she hoped no one was at home.

There was little chance that would be the case, though.

Fuck.

18

"This had to be one of the longest days in the history of days," Parker joked.

Wade snickered, agreeing. He took a sip from one of the ice-cold beers Maddy had brought out in a cooler with nothing but ice and long-neck bottles.

His future sister-in-law was definitely a keeper.

Wade was drained from the hard day. Drinking cold beers with his brother was the perfect way to end it. They were perched on the fence near the Blazing Eagle Ranch sign. Some days, he and his brothers came out here to take in all that their family had worked so hard for.

The sign meant something to all of them.

There were plenty of days they would come out here to talk about nothing, and just kick back, enjoying the beauty of the land.

Wade took a long pull from his bottle and thought

back to that morning. The doctor had worked on Sara, and just like he'd said, she was acting much better. They reunited her with her calf.

That was one disaster they were able to avoid.

"The wedding is going to be here soon," Wade remarked.

Parker and Maddy were going to get married at Blazing Eagle, the official day rapidly approaching. Apparently, they both wanted to tie the knot before the next addition of the family was born.

"I know. Hell, if it was up to me, we would have just gone down to the courthouse," Parker chuckled. "But Maddy girl wants the whole thing. An outdoor country wedding."

"At least we don't have to wear tuxedos," Wade retorted.

They clinked their glasses to that. Neither of them liked wearing suits. Hell, even to their mother's funeral, they'd worn jeans, dark shirts, and boots. It was an even bigger shock that Parker had taken off his hat to bury their momma.

"That, we do not." Parker grinned. "But honestly, if Maddy had wanted it, I would have done it."

It was no question that Parker was head over heels in love with Maddy. There wasn't anything his older brother wouldn't do for the mother of his children.

"Yeah, I know. I'm just glad she didn't." Wade finished off the beer and tossed the bottle onto the grass in front of the cooler. Reaching for another, he popped the top off with the bottle opener on his keychain.

"Are you bringing Joy?" Parker asked.

Wade paused. He forgot about bringing a date to the wedding. But now that it was mentioned, it was without question that Joy would be his date.

"I hadn't even thought about a date," Wade admitted. "But yeah, I'll bring her. Who the hell is Carson bringing?"

Parker grimaced. "Who knows. I just hope whoever it is will be someone Momma would have approved of."

They both laughed. The women Carson messed with wouldn't be anyone worth bringing home to meet their mother if she were still alive. Their brother was certainly a Brooks man, and he loved women.

"The wedding is the easy part. Are you ready for baby number two?" Wade asked.

Parker blew out a deep breath and removed his hat. He sat it down on the ground next to him.

"Can I admit that I am more nervous about meeting this baby than when I met Tyler?"

"Really?" Wade paused and glanced at his brother. "Why is that?"

"I missed out on so much with Tyler. This baby, I'll be there from day one. I don't know nothing about babies." Parker turned to Wade. There was a hint of fear and worry in his gaze. "What if I fuck this up?"

"You won't. Maddy won't let you," Wade assured him. Maddy was a wonderful mother, and Wade knew she would help calm Parker's fears. "And neither will Tyler."

Parker nodded and finished his beer, throwing his empty bottle into their growing pile. He reached for another one and opened it.

"What's wrong with you?" Parker jerked his chin to Wade. "You've been acting weird today. I know why I'm stressed. What's your problem?"

Wade snickered. It was like his brother to sniff out when something was wrong with him. The three of them were close, and were always able to speak with each other when something was bothering them.

He took his time trying to get his thoughts together before answering.

"I normally don't listen to gossip, but something has been on my mind today," Wade admitted.

He caught Parker up on the confrontation with Mike and what he'd shared with Wade and Stan. Parker remained quiet while Wade told him everything.

"But I don't know what to do. Joy isn't like her father, just as I'm not like ours. I don't think she would purposely try to deceive me to get land back."

He leaned back against the fence and stared at the sky. It was clear and picturesque. There were barely any clouds, with a few birds flying by. Even though it was later, they still had a few hours of daylight.

"Go talk with her. Don't assume nothing. Doing that will backfire on you," Parker warned. He looked away and took a gulp of his drink. "Don't be like me and lose years because of pride and shit other people said."

Wade winced.

The pain was still evident in his brother's voice. Wade didn't know what he would have done if he had been in his shoes.

The roar of an engine and tires eating up the gravel grabbed their attention. Wade turned to find a truck speeding down the road.

"Who the fuck is that?" he muttered.

"I don't know," Parker said.

Wade squinted and released a curse.

Davis Whitaker, Jr.

The truck drew to a halt, and Junior flew out. Even from where Wade was standing, he could see Junior was in a rage.

"You son of bitch!" Junior hollered.

Wade and Parker stood simultaneously, dropping their bottles to the ground.

"What the hell do you want?" Parker asked. His voice was low, but Wade knew his brother. This was the calm before the storm.

"Your brother has been fucking my sister." Junior pointed to Wade. "Y'all Brooks are done taking everything from my family. I'll be damned if you use my sister."

"What the fuck are you talking about?" Wade snapped. He wasn't going to back down from the man. Junior didn't know what he was talking about, and he was not going to come on their land accusing them of anything.

Junior had been a thorn in Wade's and his brothers' sides for a long time. The guy just couldn't leave well enough alone. He'd been badmouthing their family for years.

"Now, hold on, Junior. No one has forced anything with Joy. She and Wade's relationship is no one's business." Parker tried to be the voice of reason, but Wade could see he was holding back.

"Ain't no one talking to you, Parker," Junior snarled.

"Junior, I don't know what you think you know—"

Wade's words were cut short from Junior's fist landing a solid punch.

Wade's temper exploded.

With a roar, he swung back, his fist landing in Junior's side. He rushed Junior, not allowing him to regain his bearings.

The Brooks siblings were accustomed to having to defend each other and themselves. He was certainly not going to back down from Junior.

"Hold on a damn minute!" Parker hollered.

Wade wasn't listening to his brother. If Junior wanted a piece of him, then he was going to get what he wished for.

Junior landed another one, but Wade countered with his own. His knuckles slammed into the side of Junior's face.

"Please, don't!" Joy screamed.

Hearing her voice startled Wade. He hadn't seen her arrive.

Junior took advantage of the distraction and landed a hook to Wade's abdomen. The air rushed from his lungs with the force of the blow.

Joy ran over to Wade's side.

"Oh my God, Wade. Are you okay?" she cried out.

Wade stood up straight. He swayed and dragged in a deep breath. Wiping his mouth with the back of his hand, he saw a small smear of blood.

"I'm doing fine, baby." He looked down and saw the worry in her eyes.

She wrapped her arm around his waist. The feeling of her pressed against him calmed him. He didn't want her to see him this way, but there was nothing he could do about it now.

"Get away from him, Joy," Junior ordered. He paced back and forth like a caged animal, glaring at them. "I can't believe you're spreading your legs for the fucking enemy."

"Shut up, Junior!" she hollered.

"Brooks are liars and thieves," Junior continued.

Wade tightened his arm around Joy's shoulders. His rage was growing as he listened to Junior spout his lies.

"Junior, stop. You don't know what you're talking about," Joy sniffed, leaning her head against Wade's chest.

He bent down and breathed in the scent of her dark hair. Just holding her was comforting to him. He glared at Junior.

Did the guy ever shut the fuck up?

"I don't? Ask your little boyfriend about last year when Dad approached their father about our land, trying to strike a deal with him. Jonah literally spat in Dad's face." Junior paused his pacing and faced them with his hands resting on his hips. His eyes were feral, and his gaze landed on Wade before they switched to his sister. "You are now sleeping with his son. You need to decide which side of the fence you're going to be on, because you cannot sit on it."

Joy stiffened.

Wade bit back a curse. The son of a bitch was playing the family loyalty card.

Joy turned to him and took a step back.

"Is that true?" she asked quietly.

He could see the walls going up in her eyes.

"I don't know nothing about that." And that was the truth. His father didn't have to tell him or his brothers of any dealings or encounters. As long as he had breath in his body, he was the sole owner of the ranch.

In the back of his mind, he couldn't help but hear what Mike had said.

"I can't tell you how many times he'd rant and rave about the Brooks family, and how y'all are land thieves who break deals."

Doubts crept up inside of Wade.

If her father had been trying to get the land back, did Mike's words have some merit?

Was she playing him?

No.

There was no way the chemistry between them could have been faked.

"He's lying, Joy." Junior's voice broke through Wade's thoughts.

He focused on Joy's brother. Wade's hands clenched into fists again. He wanted to feel them land straight into Junior's mouth to shut him up.

"Watch it, now," Parker said. "You are not going to come onto our land—"

Junior pointed his finger at Parker. "You ain't no good either. We all heard what you did to Maddy. She was way too forgiving for your sorry ass."

"Fuck you." Parker moved toward Junior, but Joy jumped between them.

"Stop!" she screamed, tears flowing down her face.

Wade's heart stuttered at the sight.

"Please, just stop."

Parker glared at Junior.

"Let's go, Joy. Now," Junior demanded.

She looked to Wade, but he didn't know what to do. He didn't want to come between her and her family.

They would have to have a long talk, but now wasn't the time. They had known eventually they would have to come clean with her family and his father. Wade didn't know what had led to Junior taking off and coming to their ranch, but he was going to assume her family knew now.

"Go ahead, Joy. Go home," he said in the softest tone he could muster.

Wade was gutted, watching her face fall and her shoulders droop.

It was as if the fight had left her.

She appeared defeated.

He wanted to scream and yell for her to come to him, to take her back to his house, but he couldn't.

He refused to make her pick a side.

That was what her brother was making her do.

Didn't Junior see how it was affecting her? It was obvious he didn't care. All that mattered to Junior was the damn feud and keeping the line drawn between the Whitakers and Brooks.

Wade and Joy were grown, and what they did with each other shouldn't matter to anyone else.

"Let's go, Joy," Junior repeated, his expression smug. He grinned, even with his busted lip.

Wade narrowed his gaze on him, wanting to punch him in the throat and wipe that damn smile from his lips.

"I'll call you later." Wade ran a frustrated hand through his hair.

She nodded and walked backward, not taking her gaze from his, until finally, she turned around and followed him.

Wade wanted to run after her, but he stood frozen, watching her leave, taking his heart with her.

———

After arriving home from the brawl between Wade and Junior, Joy had locked herself in her bedroom. She couldn't look at her family.

They had all betrayed her.

She rolled over in her bed and held her pillow tight to her chest. She had laid across her mattress, and had apparently fallen asleep.

She hated when she got angry to the point of crying.

The drive back home had been torturous. One look at Wade, and she could see he was torn.

Walking away from him had been the hardest thing she'd ever done. She had wanted to run to him and never leave.

But she found herself getting back inside her truck and taking the winding road back to the Fox Run.

Glancing down at her watch, she saw it was close to midnight.

She couldn't believe what had happened.

Her eyes were gritty from crying. She was frustrated with how her family reacted. Even though her father appeared to understand, he didn't do anything to keep Junior from going to Blazing Eagle.

Didn't they know she could make her own decisions? Shouldn't they trust that she had a good head on her shoulders?

Maybe she needed to get out of the house and find her own place to stay.

Shady Springs had a few developments for the younger population. They were trying to attract families to settle there.

At her age, it was time she moved on. She couldn't expect to live with her parents forever. She'd save her money. She hadn't been mentally ready to buy, but maybe she would look for an apartment, or even a condo.

This wasn't a rash decision.

It was something she knew she needed to do, and this would be the push to finally do it.

Feeling better about herself, she swung her legs to the side of the bed. She paused there and breathed in deeply. In the morning, she would leave and go see what was available in the new part of town where they had been expanding and building a new development.

Her stomach grumbled, and she realized she hadn't eaten since lunch.

Standing, she moved over to the closet. It was then

she clocked that someone had come in and placed her bags from her shopping trip inside her room.

Joy walked over to them and picked them up. She carefully removed her purchases and put them away before changing out of her clothes. Pulling out a pair of sleep shorts and a tank, she slid them on.

Joy walked over to her door and pressed her ear to it. She didn't feel like confronting her parents at this time of night.

Not hearing anything, she opened the door.

She jumped back at the sight of Lacey, Minnie, and Duke all cuddled outside her door. They all looked up at her.

They whined and sat up.

"Shh..." she whispered, holding a finger to her lips. She stepped over them while trying not to fall on her face. She turned and held her hand up. "Stay."

She took a step back, and for once, the dogs obeyed.

They must be tired. They flopped back down on the floor.

Breathing a sigh of relief, Joy walked down the hall and headed downstairs. At this time of night, she was sure her parents would be asleep.

She entered the kitchen and beelined for the fridge. She riffled through it, and saw a bowl of tuna fish for sandwiches. Her mother's tuna fish was legendary. She did a little dance and pulled the bowl from the refrigerator.

Bread.

Turning to grab it, she yelped, finding her brother standing in the doorway. She stiffened and spun away from him.

"What are you doing?" Junior asked.

Joy rolled her eyes. Padding over to the counter, she placed the bowl down so she could gather the rest of the items she needed.

"Making myself something to eat." She continued to ignore him as she stood there scooping out tuna and spreading it over two slices of bread. If it wasn't so late, she'd make a tuna melt. But for now, a regular sandwich would do.

A pile of chips, and her late-night dinner was complete.

He didn't say a word, but she could feel his eyes on her.

Pissed was an understatement of what she was feeling toward her brother. He had crossed a line. She wasn't sure why he was still at the house, since he had his own place. Once in a while he stayed over if he planned to get up early to work.

The sound of his sigh filled the air.

She tensed when he shifted to stand next to her.

"You can't stay mad at me forever," he said, nudging her with his elbow.

Joy snorted. Apparently, her brother didn't know her that well if he thought that.

She moved to put the items away, but he grabbed her arm.

She glared at him.

"Look, I know you don't understand, but it's my job to protect you," he began. "The Brookses can't be trusted. Wade is using you. Can't you see it?"

"For the last time, Davis Whitaker, Jr., he's not." She stood close to him so he could see her eyes. She glared up at her older brother. "What's between Wade and I is none of yours or our parents' business."

"Even after hearing how Jonah basically spat in Dad's face last year, you're still taking his side?" He shook his head again and released her. "The town's nose is stuck so far up the Brookses asses, no one can see them for what they truly are."

"And what is that, Junior?" She tossed the bowl of tuna back into the fridge. She spun around and folded her arms.

"They are manipulators. They're selfish. Their business sense is shrewd, and they couldn't give a shit about the little farmers in the area." Junior stepped close to Joy. His eyes softened, and he reached out and laid his hands on her shoulders. "They use women.

You heard what Parker did to Maddy. The poor girl struggled raising their son alone, while Parker got to live the high life. Now he wants to step up? Is that the type of family you want to associate yourself with? Trust them if you want, but those Brookses are no different than their daddy. Don't be fooled."

"Wade isn't his father, and he certainly isn't his brother," she snapped. "If Maddy forgave Parker, who cares? That's their life. And when did you start listening to gossip?" She brushed past him and picked up her food. She walked over to the table and sat down.

"I'm just asking for you to trust me as your brother. You know I love you, and would go to the ends of the earth for you and Lexi. They've done enough to our family. I know how stubborn you are, but I'm just asking for you to listen to me. That's all." His voice softened.

She turned to him and looked him in the eye. He was right. She and Lexi had spent their entire lives having him protect them. In the back of her mind, she knew he was just doing the same thing, and it was actually heartwarming to know how much her brother loved her, and was willing to fight for her honor.

Her heart, on the other hand, believed in Wade and what was between them. She was in love with him, and she knew he had feelings for her too.

"Okay, I will listen." That was the only deal she

was willing to make at this point. She'd listen, but she would still make her own decisions when it came to her relationship with Wade.

"The Country Festival is this weekend. Wanna go with us?" Junior sat next to her and stole a chip from her plate.

She stared at him. It would be nice to go out and just relax with her siblings.

"Who all is going?" She took a bite of her sandwich, and just as she knew it would be, it was delicious.

"Mark, Sean, Lexi, me, and you, if you're interested." His best friends, along with their sister. It sounded like the normal crew when they went out.

She needed something to take her mind off all the craziness.

She was going to have to really think about Wade and her. She loved him, but maybe they'd rushed into everything. It might help if they stepped back and assessed what this thing between them was.

They could breathe for a moment, and really think about what they wanted. They hadn't mentioned the L word to each other.

Her heart hurt, but it was going to be what was best. She was going to have to put that old saying to the test.

If you love something, set it free. If it returns, it was meant to be...

She didn't even want to think of if he didn't return to her. Joy had a lot to work on with herself, and she needed a clear mind. Her parents weren't going to like her moving out, but they didn't have a say on that matter.

She was going to have to get herself together.

She smiled. "Sounds fun. I'm in."

Junior grinned and took another chip.

"Hey! If you are hungry, go make your own plate."

Wade was nervous as hell. He couldn't ever remember feeling this way before. He had invited Joy to meet him, just to talk. They needed to speak face-to-face about recent events.

He wanted to get everything out on the table and clear the air.

The past couple of days had been torture.

He couldn't concentrate; he didn't have a taste for any food.

Wade needed to see Joy, hold her, and tell everyone to fuck off.

He loved her.

He paused, welcoming the emotions that flooded him.

"I love Joy Whitaker," he said aloud to the world. It felt good, the words flowing off his tongue. A grin spread with the realization that he was in love.

They had agreed to meet by a large oak tree that

was on the border of her family's land and his. He had driven one of the ranch's ATVs out to the spot, and had even brought brought a blanket for them to sit on. Taking a seat, he placed his wide-brimmed hat next to him. The tree provided a good amount of shade from the sun. Resting his arms on his knees, he leaned back, waiting for her to arrive.

A few minutes later, the sound of hooves met him. He turned to find Joy atop a beautiful chestnut mare. The woman looked as if she were made to ride horses.

Wade couldn't tear his eyes away from her. Joy's dark hair flowed in the wind. She came to a stop, dismounted, and allowed her horse to graze. Wade stood as she walked toward him. He met her and took her all in.

Her beauty took his breath away.

"How do you know about this spot?" she asked. Joy was dressed in tight jeans, a white shirt tied into a knot at her stomach, and tan boots with a heel.

Wade's gaze was locked on the smooth brown skin peeking out from under her shirt.

"I come out here all the time," he admitted. He glanced around and eyed the scenery surrounding them. "It's beautiful out here. How could I not know about it?"

"Seriously?" she shook her head.

"What's wrong?" he asked, not following her.

"Nothing. It's just that this is my favorite spot. I come here when I need to get away and think." She waved for him to walk with her to the tree.

They took a seat next to each other on the blanket in the shade.

Wade wanted to touch her, but he held back. He didn't like this feeling of unrest between them. Everything had been going great until her family had intervened. That damn feud was tearing them apart, and he didn't like it.

"How are you, babe?" he asked. It was safe to start there.

She looked good. It had been two days since he'd last seen her. Unfortunately, it was in the midst of him fighting her brother.

Her brown-eyed gaze landed on him. She studied him before jerking her head in a nod. She shifted on the blanket and folded her legs underneath her.

"I'm sorry my brother punched you," she murmured.

Wade unconsciously rubbed his jaw where Junior's fist had landed. It had been a solid punch, and had Wade seeing stars for a few seconds.

"I'll be fine." Wade shook his head and waved it off. "So, I take it your family knows about us?"

"Yeah, they know."

Wade didn't like how the conversation was stilted

between them. It was as if that line was drawn between them.

"This is all my fault," he began. He turned and took her hand in his. There was no way he'd sit this close and not touch her. The scent of her perfume was teasing him.

"What are you talking about?" Joy tilted her head to the side while studying him. Her eyes were wide as she waited for him to continue.

"I should have walked my ass over to your house and spoke with your father, man to man. I could have told him how much I like you, and love being with you. I should have asked to court you."

"Court me?" Her nose wrinkled up. "What is this, the eighteen hundreds?"

He laughed. "You know what I mean."

A smile played on her lips. He ached to yank her to him so he could taste them, but he resisted. They needed to have this conversation. It was too important.

"We should have been up front with our parents, and maybe this all wouldn't have happened," he said.

"You don't know my brother like I do. It would have happened eventually," she whispered.

No longer able to resist, he pulled her to him and tilted her chin up. "Then your brother and I would have fought earlier and got it out the way."

He bent down and covered her lips with his.

The kiss was tender, slow.

Joy slid her hands up his chest, and they dove into his hair. He loved the feeling of her running her hands through his thick strands and pulling on them. He needed to have her closer.

He tugged again and assisted her onto his lap so she straddled him. His hands were once again filled with her delectable bottom. The kiss grew deeper. His cock pushed against his jeans, demanding to be let out.

Wade slipped his hand underneath Joy's shirt. It connected with her bra, and he had it unhooked in seconds.

Tearing his lips from hers, he pushed her shift up to free her beautiful mounds from the sexy lace contraption. Her nipples drew into tight buds. He captured the first one with his mouth.

Her skin was soft and sweet as his tongue played with her little bud. He drew her breast deeper into his mouth, suckling it like a starving man.

It had been a few days since he'd gotten to push deep inside her, and he was aching to do so now.

Joy gasped, threading her fingers back into his hair as if to hold in him place.

She rocked her hips against his waist, driving him crazy.

He teased her with his teeth.

His other hand dropped down to the waistband of her pants.

"Wade, wait. We shouldn't." Joy's voice broke through his lust-filled haze.

He released her breast from his mouth and looked up to meet her gaze.

"What's wrong?" he asked, his breathing rapid. No one was around, and he highly doubted anyone would come searching for them.

Joy gulped and pulled her shirt down, covering herself.

"A lot is going on," she breathed. Joy cupped his face and placed a small kiss on his lips. "My family—"

"I don't care what your family thinks, Joy." He cut her off, instantly growing irritated that her family kept butting in. "This is between you and me. Nothing can change that."

She slid off his lap and fixed her bra.

"I know that," she whispered. "I just don't want anyone to get hurt."

"Who would get hurt by us being together?" he demanded. He was losing control of the situation, and didn't like the feeling of helplessness. Joy was growing skittish right before his eyes, and he didn't know what he had done.

She stood and took a step away from him. Wade stood, watching her turn, putting her back to him. He tried to beat down his anxiety, but was losing the battle.

She swung around to face him. "Everything between us moved so fast."

"Joy, we've known each other for years." He stalked over and stopped before her. "You know you felt the same attraction between us. This has been building for a long time." He took her chin and forced her to look him in the eye.

He didn't know why, but he knew he wasn't going to like what transpired here today.

"Tell me you felt it," he whispered.

Tears formed in her eyes, spilling out onto her flawless skin. His heart slammed into his chest. He couldn't stand the sight of her crying.

"I did."

"Then how did we rush anything?" he asked softly. He didn't want to be the one responsible for her tears. He gently caressed her skin, wiping the warm streaks from her face.

"Don't think of anyone else but us, Joy."

"I am," she replied. Her voice was just a decibel over a whisper. "And that's why this is so hard."

The floor of Wade's stomach gave out. Dread immediately filled him.

"Baby, what are you talking about?" He wasn't understanding what she was trying to say.

"I think we need to take a break from each other."

Wade's breath left him. It was as if a two-by-four had slammed across his solar plexus.

"A break?" he echoed.

She gripped his shirt in her hands. "This was a difficult decision for me to make."

Wade swallowed hard.

"We both have to think about what is best for us and our families," Joy stressed.

"So, you're breaking up with me because of our families?" A dry chuckle escaped him.

Ain't this a bitch.

There was nothing funny about the situation, but it was either that or scream.

Wade reached down and gently pried her hands from his shirt before stepping away from her. He couldn't believe it.

Their fucking families.

Everything they had between them was going down the fucking drain because her family couldn't get over something that happened over thirty years ago.

She was openly crying now. "Wade, it's not like that. I'm just saying, I need time."

He shoved a hand through his hair. She took a step toward him, but he backed away with his hands up, palms facing her.

"Yeah, I hear you. Don't worry, I'll give you all the

space you want." He turned and scooped up his hat from the blanket, his feet carrying him over to the ATV.

He was a fool to think he could have something with her.

Why had he thought they would be able to over-come something that had plagued their families for decades?

"Wade!" she called out after him.

He ignored her, and the sounds of her sobs. He didn't look at her as he got in the small vehicle. If he did, he would be running back to her. Instead, he kept his eyes averted while he cranked the engine. He spun it around and drove off.

He went straight home. He was in no condition to go anywhere else.

He was left feeling raw on the inside.

Joy didn't want to be with him.

She'd broken it off.

His chest burned from the lack of air. He breathed in deeply, trying to get air inside his lungs. Wade tight-ened his hand on the steering wheel and guided the ATV in the direction of his home.

His mind was slowly processing everything that had just happened.

He pushed his foot down on the pedal. He wasn't going to be in any condition to speak with anyone.

At the moment, he wanted to drive his fist into someone's face.

Or a fucking wall.

He didn't see any of the scenery, but somehow, he made it home without crashing.

His body was running on autopilot.

Parking the ATV near his house, he killed the engine. Getting out of the vehicle, he walked to his porch, took a seat on the steps, and snatched the hat off his head.

What had truly gone wrong between them?

He was at a loss for words.

She wanted time away from him.

He had thought the bond between them was stronger, but apparently, he was wrong. There was no question that he was willing to fight for them.

But, it would seem, she was not.

Joy was numb on the inside. She was running on auto. There was no pleasure. She couldn't remember the last time she'd smiled. Leaning against the fence, she watched the sheep graze. They were lucky animals. They didn't have a care in the world.

Well, except the occasional coyote trying to come onto the land and steal one away.

It had practically broken her heart to have to tell Wade she needed space.

She'd seen the frustration in his eyes, but the second his emotions left, she'd broken down.

He had shut down.

The memory of him backing away from her cut her like a knife.

She had thought long and hard about it, and felt they needed to let things cool between them to allow everyone to come to terms with their relationship.

Just as she hadn't spoken with her father, he hadn't

shared their relationship with his. It was easy for him not to care what his father thought.

But her family, they were close-knit, and they mattered to her.

Of course, his brothers knew of them, but she wanted them to be in a place where they were open with everyone.

Even Jonah.

Was it so wrong that she now saw the error of their ways? Yes, they were both grown, but it would be selfish of them to only think of themselves and not the people who loved them.

That fight between Wade and Junior was too much for her. Both of them were stubborn men.

Hell, if she didn't get control of this, they would be coming to blows again, and next time, it could be worse.

She knew Wade.

Those damn Brooks men loved a good scrap. Hell, her brother was no different. Instead of talking like civilized men, they had to talk with their fists.

The dogs barking brought her out of her daydream. She looked over her shoulder and saw her mother walking toward her. She stiffened and turned back to her sheep watching.

"Hey, Momma," she greeted Georgy when she stood beside her. No matter how old she was, she was still going to be respectful to her mother. She hadn't informed her parents of her plans yet. She had called around and found a few apartments that were available in the new development in town in her price range. It would allow her to still work the farm, but be close enough to drive back to town to go home.

She had an appointment next week to go see them.

It was the first major step she'd made since making up her mind, and she was going to follow through with it.

"You all right, baby?" Georgy asked.

She really hadn't spoken with anyone in her family since the blowup.

Joy was hurt by everyone. It wasn't fair that she had to make the decisions she had, but she guessed it was the universe's way of telling her to get herself together.

After she got her place, she was going to try to talk with Wade again. She couldn't stand not talking with him. It had become routine for her to spend every hour she wasn't working with him.

Now, without him, she felt hollow.

"Yeah. Why do you ask?" Joy tried to keep the sarcasm from her voice, but she wasn't sure how successful she was. She didn't want to go into details about how she had torn her heart out of her chest when she'd broken it off with Wade.

"Well, I haven't seen you mope around this place

with your lip on the ground since you were ten, and we took your dirt bike away."

Joy nodded. "I'm fine. Just got some stuff on my mind."

A sheep hollered, gaining her attention. One of the males was trying to mount her, and Joy couldn't tell if the sheep was happy about it or not.

Joy looked away from the lucky couple. She couldn't believe she was slightly jealous the sheep didn't have to worry about anything with her male. They could just live, and not have anyone interfering in their lives.

"That stuff wouldn't happen to be Wade Brooks, would it?" Her mother certainly didn't pull any punches. She got right to the point. "I noticed you have been coming home every night lately."

Joy fought back tears. "You always did notice everything," she muttered.

"Did he hurt you?" her mother asked.

Joy barked out a sarcastic laugh. Angrily, she wiped at the trail of tears sliding down her face. "No. Wade would never do anything to hurt me. He was perfect in every way."

The conversation wasn't one she wanted to have with her mother. Thoughts of going to stay with Lexi for a few days came to mind. She would be the perfect person for her to spill her heart out to.

Thankfully, her sister would be arriving tomorrow for the music festival. Maybe Joy would drive back with her to the city and stay with her to clear her mind.

They could go do some shopping in the city, go out to the fancy restaurants, and bond. It had been a while since they had spent some sisterly time together.

"So, then, what's the matter?" Georgy gently prodded.

Joy's stared at her in shock. Was she being facetious?

"What do you mean 'what is the matter'? Did you forget how Junior tore over there to the Brookses ranch and fought Wade just because his last name is Brooks and mine is Whitaker?"

"Of course I didn't forget. Your brother has a protective streak a mile long, and doesn't want to see a Brooks take advantage of you like they did our family." Georgy reached for Joy, but she backed away from her.

"Did you know my brother told me I had to choose between my family and the man I love?"

She bit her lip and shook her head, trying to not full-out sob. She had been doing nothing but cry lately.

She was just tired.

Tired of having to explain herself.

Tired of having to defend her feelings for a man her family apparently would never accept.

"Baby, please, don't cry." Her mother wrapped her arms around Joy, squeezing her tight.

The feeling of her mother comforting her released the floodgates. Sobs shook her as she let go.

Why did life have to be so unfair?

She shouldn't have to choose at all. Joy leaned into her mother while the pain of losing Wade racked her body.

"How did this become so messy?" Georgy wondered aloud. She rubbed Joy's back and rocked her.

The tears flowed. The memory of Wade removing her hands from him and backing away had her crying even harder.

Joy lost track of time, but finally, her sobs subsided

She breathed in deeply and pulled away from her mother.

"I'm sorry," she murmured.

"You don't have to apologize, Joy." Georgy took her by the shoulders. "I know life is hard, and we all have big decisions to make. I hate the one that you made caused you pain. I can't tell you what to do, because only you know what is best for you."

"I don't want anyone hurt by me and my actions. I can't have y'all hating me because I'm in love with Wade Brooks." Joy bit her lip. There, she had said it.

This was the second time she'd admitted it aloud, and it felt damn good.

Yet, her heart was broken because she had never told him.

Instead of telling him the other day, she'd broken it off.

She had put her family between them. Even when he proclaimed that it should be just the two of them, she had pushed him away.

In the back of her mind, she wondered if he truly didn't know about Jonah brushing her father off again with the land agreement.

But then, her heart believed him, and knew he didn't have anything to do with it.

He was innocent, just as she was.

"Even if I wanted to get back with Wade, he probably wouldn't speak with me." She rubbed her face. She had hurt him.

Bad.

She had seen it right before he'd shut down on her.

Georgy ran her hand over Joy's back. "Everything will be all right. Maybe the time apart will do you some good. Maybe the fog in your brain will clear, and you can think with it instead of your other parts."

Joy snorted. She was not about to have that type of conversation with her mother.

"Mom, please don't."

"Fine," Georgy chuckled.

They grew silent while watching the sheep graze. The two who had been getting busy were now eating near each other.

It was official.

Joy was jealous of the pair.

Have sex, eat together, and then not to have to worry about anything else.

Joy shook her head.

It must be nice.

"So, have you thought about which sheep we're lending to the fair?" Georgy asked.

The annual fair was coming to town in two weeks, and the Whitakers always lent some of their sheep for the Mutton Bustin' competition. It was one of the highlights of the fair.

Little tykes riding sheep was the cutest thing Joy had ever seen. She loved to watch the five-and six-year-olds ride the sheep and compete against each other.

The kids trained hard, and took mutton bustin' seriously.

It was a big deal in Shady Springs.

Joy couldn't wait for the day where she could have children of her own. She would definitely be working with them to train and enter the games.

When Joy was younger, she was a mutton bustin'

champion. She had plenty of ribbons from her time as a youngster. It had been so much fun, and some of her fondest memories as a child were on the back of a sheep.

Images of her with a chubby, dark-haired baby with curly hair and gray eyes flashed before her, and Joy shook it off.

Those gray eyes.

Joy's heart ached.

There was no sense in fantasizing of what could have been.

She may have ruined whatever future she had with Wade.

"When do they need them delivered?" Georgy asked, breaking into her fantasy.

"The morning of the event."

"Well, come on, dear. Let's go get dinner started." Her mother wrapped an arm around her and pulled her toward the house.

"What to wear?" Joy stared at the clothing hanging in her closet. She tightened the towel around her and blew out a deep breath. Today they were going to the Country Festival, and her sister was in her room getting prepped. Junior would be picking them up in about an hour, and she had yet to figure out what outfit to wear.

A knock sounded at the door. It flew open, followed by a gasp.

"You're not dressed yet?"

Joy glanced over her shoulder and shrugged. "Too many choices?"

Lexi giggled. "What am I going to do with you?" Rushing across the room, she joined Joy in front of the closet, riffling through the items before them. "For you to still be a country bumpkin, you sure do have a lot of clothes."

"What can I say?" Joy murmured. She turned around and walked over to her bed. Taking a seat, she decided to let Lexi pick something out for her. Lexi had a good eye for fashion.

It wasn't like Joy was trying to catch anyone's eye.

The only person she would want to dress up for probably wouldn't even speak to her.

Lexi spun around with a few outfits in her hands. One look at Joy, and her smile disappeared.

"Oh, sis. It's going to be okay." She came and sat next to Joy, tossing the clothes on the bed.

Lexi had arrived last night, and they had stayed up late drinking wine and watching movies, while Joy brought her up to speed on everything that had gone down with Wade.

Lexi had listened to her, and there was no judgement. Just a sympathetic ear for Joy to share her feelings.

"I don't think so. I really hurt him," she whispered. Joy took her hand and entwined their fingers.

"Well, I think your idea of coming back to the city with me is a fine one. I have some time I can take from work, and we can just relax together. There's plenty for us to do."

When Joy had asked about coming to stay with her for a few days, Lexi was immediately on board.

"Thanks, sis." She knew she would be able to count on Lexi. Getting away from Shady Springs was going to help her clear her mind and get her life together. She needed a distraction. If she stayed on the ranch, she would just continue to think of Wade, who was one ranch over.

"Now, let's get you dressed and do something with your hair. We are not going to think of men." Lexi squeezed her hand and grinned. "We are going to have some fun listening to some good country music and day drinking, that will obviously go on into the night."

Joy laughed. "You know I don't drink like that." A few glasses of wine, she could handle, but hard liquor always knocked her on her ass.

The Country Festival was known for its big party atmosphere. Three days' worth of concerts had people coming from all over. All of the top country stars, as well as rising ones, came to perform. There would be tons of food and booze for people to have a good time.

"Oh, this occasion calls for us to drink," Lexi stated matter-of-factly. She stood and snagged the clothes from the bed. She held them up to show Joy what she had chosen. "Get dressed."

"Eliana, thanks for coming to stay the night," Wade said, leaning against the doorframe to the kitchen.

His father's nurse spun around with a wide grin. "It's no problem, Wade. You fellas deserve to have one night out to relax and be young." She moved over to the stove and lifted the lid to a pot, stirring the contents. From the scent floating through the air, she was making chili.

It was one of his father's favorites. Jonah Brooks could eat chili all year long.

Wade snorted. He wasn't in any mood to go out with his brothers, but they weren't hearing of him staying home.

The country music festival was a big event, and his brothers were determined to take him with them. Parker was bringing Maddy along, while Tyler went to stay with Maddy's mother for the weekend.

Apparently, Parker and Maddy were taking full advantage of being childless this weekend.

"I'll go check on Pa before I leave," he offered.

"Oh, he will behave, don't you worry. I don't put up with Jonah's shit," Eliana vowed.

"Yes, ma'am," Wade chuckled, pushing off the doorframe. Turning, he walked down the hall to the family room.

This had been the house he and his brothers had grown up in. Even though it had been years since his mother died, Jonah refused to remove any of the reminders of Grace from the house.

Wade entered the large room with vaulted ceilings. His father was settled in an oversized recliner, watching an old black-and-white Western movie. Jonah loved the Old West, and Wade had plenty of memories of walking in this same room to find Jonah and his mother sitting together on the couch, their attention on the television while an old-fashioned shootout played across the screen.

Jonah would have a drink and his famous cigarette in hand while Grace was cuddled underneath his arm.

Jonah wasn't an affectionate man, but for Grace, he would have done anything.

Wade shook the memory from his mind.

Jonah's sharp eyes watched Wade as he ambled across the room.

"You doing good, Pa?" Wade asked. He went straight for the bar and took out a glass. If he was going to have to go out with his brothers, then he was going to ensure he had a good time.

He had caught Parker and Carson up on Joy breaking things off with him. He hadn't gone into much detail, just the most important thing. She didn't want to be with him.

She didn't trust him, and didn't believe in them enough to even try.

She'd just given up.

Browsing through the bottles, he picked up his favorite whiskey and poured a double.

"What's got you drinking, boy?" Jonah asked.

Wade took a gulp and turned. The amber liquid burned going down. It was a good choice brand. His father had always kept the best liquor in the house.

When Wade was about fifteen or so, he and his brothers had snuck into his father's liquor cabinet and stolen a fine bottle of alcohol. They had given the excuse of going out fishing at the creek late at night.

They had done it before just to have fun.

This time, they had a full bottle of booze.

They had drunk the entire bottle and had gotten shit-faced that night.

Jonah had found out, and, of course, the bottle they stole had been one hell of an expensive one.

There was no punishment needed.

Jonah had ridden out to the creek and collected them. He had been pissed, but he hadn't said a word. Wade, Parker, and Carson were so damn sick. They all had thrown up at least twice on the ride home.

Each of the boys had been hungover, but Jonah hadn't shown them any mercy.

At five in the morning, he had them up doing chores.

"Real men who go out drinking all night still get up for work in the morning."

Jonah's dry chuckle still echoed in Wade's head as he'd dragged his boys out to the barn. Carson had it the worst. He hadn't even made it halfway there before falling on his knees and puking again.

Those were the good ol' days.

He and his brothers always stuck together. There were countless memories of their shenanigans.

"Going to the festival." Wade shrugged nonchalantly. He leaned back against the bar and met his father's eyes.

Jonah turned down the volume on the television. "If I didn't know any better, I would say you were having woman troubles."

Wade snorted. That was an understatement. He knocked back more of the whiskey.

"Don't want to get into that," Wade muttered.

Jonah huffed. He stared at Wade, adjusting his chair to bring up the legs.

"That Whitaker gal giving you trouble?"

Wade jerked, almost dropping his glass. His gaze widened as he stared at his father.

What the hell?

How did the old man know about Joy?

"Don't think because I'm cooped up in the house most of the time that I don't know what is going on around here." Jonah shook his head and ran a hand across his jaw. "There isn't anything that goes on at the Blazing Eagle that escapes me."

"I guess the gossip mill has been talking." He had fleeting thoughts of Mike, and wondered if he had been the one to tell his father. He would rather have someone say shit to his face instead of whispering it behind his back.

"Gossip is shit that ain't true. Were you messing with the Whitaker girl or not?" his father asked.

He swirled the amber liquid around in his glass and pondered the question. To Wade, it was more than just "messing around." He'd thought they had something good going on between them.

"Yeah," Wade admitted. He might as well tell the truth.

"Hell, a blind man could see the way she was

looking at you that night at dinner," Jonah said. "I'm getting old, not senile."

"Well, you don't have to worry about anything. She broke it off." Just saying it out loud had Wade getting pissed again.

The hurt and rage he harbored inside of him was aching to burst out.

After that day he'd walked away from her, he'd thrown himself into the ranch. He had been working from before the sun came up to well after it went down.

Wade would go home, shower, and ate nothing before falling asleep. Most times, he woke up on the couch. It was too hard to sleep in the bed they'd made love in more times than he could count. Her scent was still on his sheets.

The sounds of her sobs still haunted him.

Jonah smirked. "I'm not even sure how the two of you got involved with each other. I'm sure her father had a shit fit over a Brooks sleeping with his daughter."

Wade stared at his father. The question was burning inside him.

"Did Senior come to you and ask to buy their land back?" The alcohol was doing all the talking. Normally, Wade didn't get involved with the business dealings of the ranch.

But he had to know.

Since it was assumed he knew, he might as well find out what really happened.

Jonah stared off toward the television. Wade couldn't tell if he was really watching it. Was the old man going to just ignore his question?

"Senior came by one day." Johan looked older than his sixty years. Life as a rancher wasn't easy for the man. "He came by demanding the land his family had sold to my grandfather. But, as you know, we've already cultivated that land, and selling that parcel back to him would be impossible."

Wade's house was built on the part of Blazing Eagle that was formally Fox Run.

"What happened?" Wade asked.

"Well, I offered another section that was still neighboring them, but it wasn't what they wanted. Senior wanted the creek, and that would never be a part of the sale." Jonah's face hardened.

Even Wade knew that would have been a bad deal for them. The creek was a natural resource, and it was vital for their property and the animals.

"The son of a bitch wouldn't take what I had offered, and what he had laid on the table for the creek was only a tenth of what it would be worth. I don't bite my tongue, and told him where he could stuff his offer."

Two stubborn old men who couldn't reach an

agreement. There were always three sides of a story, Wade knew.

Senior's version, Jonah's, and then God above.

He finished off the whiskey and poured himself another hefty glass.

"Go easy now, boy. How are you going to enjoy a music festival if you're too drunk?" Jonah questioned.

"I'll be fine," Wade snapped, spinning back around to face his father. "Eliana is staying the night. Don't give her no shit while we're gone."

He could feel the effects of the alcohol already. His father just stared at him without a snarky reply.

Good.

Sometimes, being firm with the old man was the only way to get through that thick skull of his. After the heart attack, he must have learned to choose his battles wisely. He didn't argue with them as much as he used to.

Wade took another gulp, and put the bottle back in the case.

"You're not driving, are you?" Jonah asked.

Wade chuckled.

Now, a concerned Jonah was new. His father had never shown it before. Even after their mother died, it was like Jonah had forgotten about his children.

The old man had taken his wife's death hard.

The boys had needed their father's strength and comfort, but it had never come.

Parker, Wade, and Carson had to be there for each other, and Parker stepped in for them. They had been young men in high school and middle school when Grace died. Jonah had thrown himself into the ranch, and had expected the boys to do the same.

There was a missing hole in all their hearts.

The death of their mother was what kept the boys as close as they were. There was an unspoken vow amongst them that they would always stand beside each other.

"Nope." Wade faced his father. "Parker's bringing Maddy, so by default, they are the designated drivers."

His phone buzzed in his jeans. He pulled it out and found a text from Carson.

Let's go. We're out front.

"Gotta go, Pa. They're waiting for me." Wade tipped his glass to Jonah and headed out of the room. He felt his father's gaze on him, but he refused to look back. He didn't have to worry, for he knew Eliana would have everything handled.

"Someone pregamed," Carson announced.

Wade closed the door and leaned back in his seat, ignoring his younger brother.

"Let's go." Wade motioned to Parker, who stared at him for a moment, then nodded.

Parker threw the vehicle in drive and pulled off.

His older brother had purchased a larger SUV in preparation of the new baby. It was large, spacious, and had a third row.

"Nice truck," Wade said.

"Thanks," Parker replied

"I tried to tell Parker we didn't need such a big truck. I don't know if I can drive it," Maddy said. She turned around in the passenger seat and stared at him. She bit her lip and hesitated. "Are you okay? You know, you don't have to go—"

"Yes, he does," Carson interjected.

Wade's gaze cut to Carson.

"Don't look at me like that. We are going to go drinking and listen to some good ol' country music, which is exactly what you need." Carson slapped him on the knee and grinned.

"He's right," Parker agreed. His gaze met Wade's in the rearview mirror. "We are going to get you shitfaced tonight." Parker tossed him a wink, turning his attention back to the road.

"Hell yeah!" Carson hollered, pumping his fist in the air.

Wade shook his head at his brothers.

What would he do without them?

"You boys can drink all you want, just no fighting." Maggie wagged a finger at all of them.

Wade, Parker, and Carson all shared a look, then burst out into laughter.

The Brooks brothers never instigated fights. Someone always started shit with one of them.

They just happened to be really good at ending it.

"There sure are a lot of people here this year," Lexi exclaimed.

She and Joy strolled arm in arm through the crowd. The Country Festival drew a large amount of people each year it returned.

Joy glanced around and shook her head. There were so many women barely dressed, and already drunk. Lots of sexy cowboys and men walking around almost caused her sister to get whiplash.

Joy was enjoying the music and spending time with her siblings. Junior was ahead with his best friends, Mark and Sean. They had all gone to high school and junior college together.

Mark had his dark brown hair tapered on the edges, leaving the top long enough to put in a man bun. Sean, on the other hand, was a ginger. He embraced his roots and kept his auburn curls neat.

They would always tease him that in the summer,

he couldn't hang with the rest of them since he burned so easily.

Though Mark and Sean weren't black, they were still a part of their family. Race had never played a role in their relationship with Junior.

"I can't have you being a bump on a log," Lexi murmured.

"I'm okay," Joy assured her. She patted her on the arm and smiled. It wasn't her best one, but she tried to fake it. She was grateful for her siblings trying to protect her and make her feel better.

"If I don't get too drunk tonight, we'll leave to go back to my house first thing in the morning," Lexi offered.

"I'm not drinking, so I could drive," Joy mentioned.

Lexi giggled. "That would work too."

Joy knew it would, and she was looking forward to going up to the city. Her sister could sleep off her buzz while Joy drove. She had been to her sister's place quite a few times, so she wouldn't need directions.

"Let's head over to the bar," Junior suggested over his shoulder.

"Hell yeah!" Lexi shouted. She picked up speed, dragging Joy with her to catch up with Junior, Mark, and Sean.

Off in the distance, there was an enormous makeshift tent that housed a large bar and a dance floor. They stood in line for a few minutes, showed their wristbands to security, and were granted entrance.

The tent had vaulted ceilings that were decorated with white string lights. The decor was that of an old country barn, with wooden tables and stools. It was such a massive place that there were twin bars located on each side of the space.

The dance floor was packed with people doing the most current line dance. Music blared from the speakers, so loud, Joy had issues hearing herself think.

"Come, sisters. Let's go have a drink." Junior walked up behind them and wrapped his arms around their shoulders.

"I'm not really drinking tonight. Ya'll go ahead." Joy smiled. She didn't have a problem being the designated driver. They all could have a great time, and she'd make sure they each made it home safely.

"One drink. I know you can't hold your liquor well, but we are going to celebrate you kicking that loser to the side." Junior grinned.

"Junior, that is not funny," Lexi hissed. She faced him with a narrowed gaze.

Junior rolled his eyes and guided them over to where his friends had saved them chairs at the first bar.

Lexi turned a sympathetic eye to Joy as they took their seats. "Don't mind your brother."

Joy laughed dryly. "I don't half the time."

Junior got the attention of the bartender and ordered their drinks.

Lexi scooted closer to Joy, since the music appeared to get louder as the song changed.

"Are you going to be okay?

"I'll be fine. I don't want to ruin everyone's fun. But if y'all want to move on to do something else, that's fine. I can just stay here." She didn't want to kill the buzz. They were here to have fun, but she just wasn't in the mood for partying. The music was great, but she wasn't ready to party and act as if everything was okay.

"Hell no. We are not leaving you." Lexi shook her head. "There are way too many people here. We'll get lost, and there will be no telling how long it would take to find each other."

Joy smiled. Her sister was acting as if they didn't have cell phones and could call each other.

"Plus, if you need me, I'm here for you." Lexi wrapped an arm around Joy and hugged her.

"Drinks have arrived," Junior announced. He helped the bartender pass out the shots. Junior stepped over to Joy and placed a glass in her hand. "You are drinking this. It will help you feel better." He pressed a kiss to her forehead.

Her muscles softened, and she relaxed slightly.

Her brother could be rough around the edges, but he always meant well—in his own way.

Junior, in his usual style and fashion, got the attention of everyone around them.

"I need for everyone to hold up their glasses," he announced.

The entire bar, including Joy, did as he requested. All eyes were on him. Being the center of attention was right up Junior's alley.

"I want to make a toast. To good music, to friends—the ones you came with and the ones you meet tonight—and to one hell of a party."

"Hear, hear!" echoed around them.

Lexi turned and held her glass up to Joy. "And to getting over heartbreak."

"Ain't that the truth." Joy clinked her glass to her sister's. She knocked back the shot and set her glass down on the counter. She shook her head, feeling the burn from the vodka. A warmness spread through her belly.

Oh, she was going to be feeling the effects soon.

Junior was the life of the party. He called out for another round, but Joy shook her head no.

He ignored her, and ordered her another one.

Laughing, she turned to lean back against the bar and stared off at the crowd walking by. The atmosphere was electric. Everyone had the same goal in mind, to relax and have fun. Laughter and conversation filled the air below the music floating through the speakers.

Maybe her siblings were right.

She needed to relax, have fun, and try to get Wade Brooks out of her mind, starting tonight.

Joy glanced over at her sister and saw Lexi gazing off in the distance.

Joy nudged Lexi with her elbow. "What are you looking at so intently?"

"Nothing." Lexi was a horrible liar.

Her eyes darted back to Joy, and something was wrong. Joy could feel it.

She glanced around, but didn't see anything.

"What is wrong?" she asked again.

"Maybe we shouldn't have come." Lexi gripped her hand. "I'm so sorry, Joy."

Joy's heart raced. Now, she was getting upset.

"Lexi, stop being so weird. What the hell is the matter with you?" She pulled her hand away and stood from her seat.

Lexi closed her eyes and blew out a deep breath. She raised her hand and pointed to the corner of the other bar across the enclosure.

Dread filled Joy as she turned to follow where Lexi was pointing.

She froze.

The air was ripped from her lungs. Her gaze was locked on Wade sitting at the bar with his brother, Carson.

It wasn't the fact that they were at the bar drinking.

It was the woman hanging off of Wade.

She was a tall blonde in a short skirt and a shirt that showed off her midriff. The mystery woman was practically crawling onto his lap. She whispered something in his ear, and was rewarded with a smile from Wade.

Joy couldn't remove her eyes from the scene.

Nausea filled her.

She had to fight down the bile that threatened to come up.

Just that quick, she had been replaced.

Joy fought back tears. Her vision blurred slightly. She sniffed and tried to look away, but she couldn't.

The girl whispered something else to him, and he shook his head. The blonde ran her fingers through his hair, and Joy just about lost her battle with her drink and the food she had eaten at the festival.

Joy had loved running her hands through his thick curls.

That was her thing.

Wade would smile and lean into her hand. He had fussed about being overdue for a haircut, and she had loved how the tips of his hair curled underneath his Stetson.

"I'm sorry, sis." Lexi's voice broke through her thoughts. She rested her hand on Joy's arm.

Joy blinked and spun away from the sight.

"I'm okay," Joy tried to assure her sister. "I broke it off with him, remember?"

"If you want to leave right now, we can," Lexi offered, but Joy shook her head.

She had broken it off with Wade, and it would be unrealistic to think that they wouldn't run into each other.

"No, we do not have to leave the festival. Let's just leave here." Joy didn't want her siblings' time to be ruined because she was a mess.

Lexi hopped down from her seat. "Let's go."

Junior turned and glanced at them.

"Where are you two going?" His eyes narrowed on Joy. "What's wrong?"

"It's nothing." Joy waved a hand. She sniffed and stepped away from the bar.

"No, tell me." He stepped in front of her to block her. "You look like you are about to cry."

"Leave her alone. It's just that Wade's here." Lexi grabbed Junior's arm.

"Lexi!" Joy whirled on her sister. She brushed her hair that had fallen in her face, unable to believe her sister would tell Junior. It was like throwing gasoline on a small fire.

"Where?" Fury rolled across Junior's face.

"Look, don't worry about it. I just want to leave here and check out some of the little stores," Joy lied. The festival included not only the four stages set up for concerts, but with food and merchandise vendors with booths out on the fairgrounds.

Junior's hardened gaze searched the tent, and he must have caught sight of Wade.

"Well, ain't this a bitch. See, this is what I was talking about, Joy. That motherfucker has already moved on. And you said he cared for you?" Junior snapped. His eyes darkened as he reached up and passed a hand over his face.

Joy hated seeing her brother angry, and at the moment, he had alcohol flowing through him. The two were never a good combination.

"What's going on?" Mark asked. He was about the same size as Junior, but with wider shoulders.

Sean left his spot at the bar and joined them. "Yo, what the hell got you so pissed off?" His blue eyes darted between Joy and Junior.

"Does that look like he's thinking about you?" Junior pointed off in Wade's direction.

Sean and Mark's gazes followed his finger.

"Is that the Brooks you said you fought the other day?" Mark asked. He set his glass down on the counter.

"He was the one who had Joy crying?" Sean huffed, eyeing the other bar.

Oh, fuck.

Panic spread through Joy. This wasn't a good idea. Mark and Sean were similar to her brother. They didn't give a shit about brawling, and had tempers just as short.

Joy stepped forward and reached for her brother. She didn't want any trouble.

"Please, Junior, don't cause a scene. I just want to leave," she practically pleaded.

Junior clenched his jaw and shared a look with his friends. Mark, Sean, and Junior were extremely close, and the former were an extension of the Whitaker family. They had spent a better part of their summers at Fox Run.

"Junior, listen to Joy. We are just going to leave, that's all," Lexi stressed. "We want to go enjoy the rest of the festival."

Junior wasn't listening to either of them.

Joy glanced at Lexi.

This was not going to end well.

"You want to leave?" he asked.

Joy and Lexi both nodded. A small spark of hope filled Joy. Maybe this once they could talk Junior out of something.

"I just want to leave," Joy repeated. She reached

out and gripped her brother's arm. His muscles were taut under her touch. "Please."

He glanced at her, and the devilish glint that appeared in his eyes had that glimpse of hope fading fast.

"Fine. We'll leave, but we're going to stop over there and say hello first."

"Why don't we get out of here?" Stephanie murmured in Wade's ear.

He was trying to be nice. They had history, one that Wade wasn't interested in rekindling. They had dated a few years back when he was younger and carefree.

He had scratched a few itches for her, and she'd returned the favor. It had been a while since he had seen her. They had mutually agreed they'd had a good time between them, but the relationship wasn't going anywhere. Stephanie had been good company, but now, Wade wasn't interested at all.

Walking through the festival, they had run into each other. She and her friend, April, had attached themselves to him and Carson ever since.

"I'm good. I'm here with my brothers," Wade murmured. He took a sip of his drink and glanced over at her.

For a second, there were two of her floating along-side him. He blinked, and his vision cleared.

"That never stopped you before." Her finger stroked his hair near his ear. She pressed closer to him, her breasts brushing his arm. "We used to have fun together."

"That, we did," he agreed. He wasn't in the mood to go down memory lane. They'd had fun together, but that was in the past, and that was where it was going to stay.

Parker and Maddy had disappeared off to the dance floor. A popular song had come on that had Maddy dragging Parker off into the crowd. There were too many people, and Wade would pay to see his older brother out there cutting a rug.

None of the Brooks brothers could dance.

They couldn't be good at everything.

Stephanie was trying her best to get him to take her home, but it was not going to happen. Back in the day, he would admit the feeling of her hands running over him would get his motor running. But now, it did absolutely nothing for him.

What he missed was the creamy brown-skinned beauty who loved her sexy lingerie, riding her horse, and who had his heart.

Wade finished off his drink and set the empty glass down on the counter. He glanced at Carson, who was sitting comfortably with April in his lap. Wade stood, displacing Stephanie off of him. He turned and held up two fingers to snag the bartender's attention.

"Another round?" Wade asked Carson. He had lost track of how much he'd had to drink. He swayed slightly, but he would be fine.

Hell, he was able to stand.

That was all that mattered.

"What are you drinking?" Wade asked April.

"Jack and Coke," she replied.

Wade turned to Stephanie and raised an eyebrow. "You?" he asked.

"Same." She batted her eyes at him. Her red lips spread out into a wide grin. "You should remember what I drink. Nothing's changed with me." She flipped her long hair over her shoulder.

He grunted, and bit back a snarky comment.

He'd seriously forgotten all about her until he'd laid eyes on her tonight.

Wade was feeling generous with buying drinks. After all, they were here to party and listen to good music. The plan was for him to get wasted, and that was what he was going to do.

He hoped Carson and Parker were ready to carry him home.

The need to have something help him bury the

hurt and pain he felt deep in his chest was present. That was where the alcohol came into play.

He was hollow on the inside without Joy.

He would drink himself into a stupor and go home. Alone.

"Yes, sir?" The bartender arrived in front of him. "What can I get you?"

Wade ordered their drinks and rested his hands on the counter. Stephanie stood next to him, dancing in place, and tried to entice him to dance with her. He shook his head, forgetting about her playful side.

Wade Brooks didn't dance.

Never had, and was never going to start.

Stephanie giggled and bumped her hip against his. He grunted, and attempted as best as he could to stand straight. The alcohol had definitely taken its toll on him. Running a hand along his face, he paused.

He would have sworn he had heard someone call out his last name over the music.

"Brooks!"

There it was again. Wade glanced at Carson, who casually slid April from this lap.

Carson grinned. "Excuse me, pretty lady."

April moved to the side to allow Carson to stand. They both turned around to see Junior Whitaker storming toward them.

"You have got to be shitting me," Carson muttered.

His smile disappeared. He glanced over at Wade, having been brought up to speed about the confrontation at the ranch by Parker after it was over.

Stephanie leaned against his arm and wrapped hers around his. She rested her head on his shoulder.

"Who is that?" she whispered.

Wade took a step forward and shook her off. If the snarl on Junior's face wasn't a clue that Junior wasn't coming over for a pleasant conversation, he didn't know what would be.

"You might want to leave now," Wade warned her. He gently pushed her away from him.

This wasn't going to be pretty. He may not want to go home with her, but he didn't want her getting hurt.

There was a resentment in Junior's eyes that Wade had seen before.

But that wasn't what caught Wade's attention.

Joy.

She was beautiful. Just one look at her had him wanting to go to her and plead for her to reconsider her decision.

She was dressed in what looked to be a one-piece short outfit that highlighted her every curve. It dipped low, showcasing her cleavage, while displaying her toned thighs. Her dark hair flowed around her shoulders.

He swallowed hard, drinking her in.

It had been a few days since he had seen her, but it felt like an eternity.

Her eyes shifted from him to Stephanie.

Shit.

This probably didn't look good.

"What the hell do you want, Junior?" Carson asked. He turned his baseball cap around so the brim was to the back.

Junior's pals flocked to both sides of him. They appeared familiar to Wade, but currently, he was too intoxicated to remember where he had seen them before.

"I'm here proving a point to my sister," Junior stated.

"Yeah, what the fuck is that?" Wade asked. He swayed and struggled to keep from toppling over. His gaze wandered back to Joy, who was standing with her sister. Her eyes were wide, and tears were streaming down her face.

He hated seeing her crying.

It ripped a bigger hole in what was left of his heart.

"Junior, let it go," Joy pleaded. She shook herself free from Lexi's hold and moved to Junior. "I told you I'm okay. Please, let's just leave."

Junior didn't take his eyes from Wade's. The people who had been sitting at the bar around Wade and Carson had cleared out.

"It would seem I'm coming back just in time for the real party," Parker drawled. He came to stand next to Wade, the spot Stephanie had vacated.

She and her friend had finally gotten the hint and scrambled away.

Parker casually leaned against the bar. Pushing his hat back, he eyed the men in front of them. "Is there a problem?"

Wade chuckled.

"I wouldn't want to ruin your date with your fiancée, big brother. Why don't you go back to Maddy."

Parker snorted. "And leave you two to have all the fun with these three fucknuts? Get the fuck out of here."

"Yeah, there's a problem," Junior barked. "Looks like your brother doesn't waste any time in between women."

"Junior, that's none of your business!" Joy shouted.

"Joy, you may want to move," Lexi hissed. She snatched Joy by the arm and dragged her out of the way.

Wade stood to his full height and rubbed his hand along his jaw. "Not that it's any of your business, but your sister broke it off with me—"

Wade's head snapped back from the force of Junior's left hook. Wade crashed into the bar.

All hell broke loose.

Parker dove after the redheaded guy. His brother may walk with a limp, but that didn't have any effect on him when it came to brawling.

Wade grinned and wiped his mouth with the back of his hand. It came away covered in his blood.

He glanced up at Junior.

Maybe this was what he needed. He had needed something to expel his feelings, and Junior was a prime candidate.

He pushed off the bar and swung his fist at Junior.

Screams went up in the air as the brawl ensued. Carson landed a solid two-piece on the dark-haired guy.

He'd lost sight of Parker, but from the ruckus sounding to his left, his brother was handling business. He didn't dare take his focus off of Junior.

The only thing Wade could hope for was that Joy was able to get to safety.

Wade stumbled, barely missing the fist going for his face, but the other connected with his side. The air escaped him. The fucker's hit felt like a damn brick slamming into his face.

Wade shoved his elbow and landed it against Junior's nose. He felt the satisfactory crunch of bone. He followed it with his own left, landing it on Junior's jaw. Wade allowed his anger and fury to consume him.

It was as if his body was overtaken by the beast

inside of him who had wanted to attack the world for taking Joy from him.

Junior was no different. They were about the same size and weight, and well-matched.

The feud between the two families was bound to explode eventually. It had only just graced the surface the other day.

At present, Wade was the right one for Junior.

Joy not being with him was the fault of the Whitakers and whatever the hell they were feeding her. He was sure it was Junior telling her some crazed bullshit that got her doubting him and everything they had between them.

Everything had been fine with them until her family had found out about them.

He didn't know what they had told her, but at the moment, Junior was going to pay.

Junior let loose a roar and rushed Wade, catching him by the waist.

"Shit," Wade muttered. The son of a bitch was as strong as an ox.

Junior slammed Wade onto a table. It splintered and crashed to the floor.

Wade paused, his back tensing from the pain radiating through him. A groan escaped him. Dirt and dust floated through the air above him.

Ringing filled his ears.

He shook it off and rolled to his side. Thick copper liquid filled his mouth. He spat it out on the floor, seeing the dark redness of his blood.

Now, he was beyond pissed.

Ignoring the throbbing of his knuckles and the scream of his back muscles, he pushed himself from the floor and turned back to Junior with his fists raised in a defensive stance.

This was nowhere near over.

"You should have stayed down, Brooks," Junior ranted.

Wade took some satisfaction in Junior's swollen, bloodied and bruised face.

"Not a fucking chance," Wade retaliated. He was a Brooks, and they didn't give up. They fought until there was no more to give.

Then they gave more.

Sirens sounded. Blue and red lights slashed through the night sky.

"Freeze!" Shouting around them grew louder. "Hands in the air!"

Wade froze. He slowly raised his hands as he was ordered. Something warm trailed down his face.

The room spun.

Wade blinked in an attempt to clear his vision.

Rough hands grabbed him and forced his arms behind him.

"You are under arrest," a voice growled.

The sheriff's department had flooded the bar with guns trained on them.

Cool metal cuffs surrounded Wade's wrists and snapped shut. They were tight, and dug into his skin.

Wade ignored the words the deputy was saying. He didn't fucking care. His gaze roamed the area in search of Joy. He needed to know she was unharmed.

But he didn't see her.

The cops dragged him toward the exit of the makeshift bar. They practically had to carry him through the thick crowd that milled around. There was a dull roar in his head.

His gaze landed on the patrol cars.

Well, shit.

This hadn't been in the plan for tonight.

The seats in the sheriff's department were hard, while the atmosphere was cold and unwelcoming. Not that Joy expected it to be plush with expensive furniture, but they could have at least offered decent coffee.

The cup sitting on the table next to her was a step above a questionable dark sludge.

"Dad, we're okay. Junior, Mark, and Sean got arrested tonight." Lexi paused and glanced at her with her phone to her ear.

Joy blew out a deep breath, knowing it was better if her sister spoke with her parents. Lexi had a way with them, making her the voice of reason.

She leaned forward and rested her head in her hands. She couldn't believe Junior had instigated another fight with Wade and his brothers. Junior was like a stubborn bull. Once he saw red, he was going to charge at the target.

Wade.

Just seeing Junior and Wade coming to blows made her sick. This was much worse than their scrap at the ranch. Tonight, they'd been truly trying to hurt each other.

"Yeah, we have enough to post for Mark and Sean too," Lexi announced.

Lexi and Joy had gotten lucky. One of the deputies had allowed them to get the keys to Junior's truck. Had he not done that, Lexi and Joy would have been stuck out at the fairgrounds.

That was one thing about living out in a small town. There was no ridesharing such as Uber. They would have had to call their father and have him drive the forty-five-minute trip to pick them up.

"Joy's right here." Lexi glanced at her.

Joy shook her head. She didn't want to speak with her parents at this time.

"I'm sure they will reimburse us, Dad. I'm not worried about that." Lexi paused and tilted her head to the side. She pulled her phone away from her head and glanced down at it. "The signal in here is horrible," she muttered. She placed her phone back to her ear. "What did you say? Hold on, I can't hear you. I'm going to step outside." Lexi pointed to the door.

Joy gave her a nod and turned to look at the deputy sitting at the counter.

She crossed her legs and settled back in her chair.

The drab area could do with some sprucing up, starting with more comfortable chairs, and some better plain color choices for the walls. A little color would go a long way.

Deputy Griffen continued working at the computer quietly. According to him, Junior, Mark, and Sean were still being processed, and they couldn't pay their bond yet until the amount was determined. They had done some true damage at the bar.

Joy had been shoved out the way the minute chairs and bodies went flying. The last thing she saw was Junior punching Wade in his face, sending him crashing back into the bar.

When would all of this fighting stop?

What would it take to settle everything between them?

A warm trail of tears slid down her cheeks. She sniffed and reached up to wipe them away. The door opened and she looked up, expecting to see Lexi walk back through it.

Instead, it was Jonah Brooks, along with the woman Joy assumed to be Eliana, his nurse. Wade had mentioned the nurse who had really been helping them with their father.

Jonah had a cane in his hand, and slowly made his way across the room. He walked over to the desk and straightened to his full height. It was uncanny how much his boys looked like him.

"Mr. Brooks, it's been a while since I've seen you here," Deputy Griffen chuckled.

Jonah released a grunt and leaned against the counter. "At my boys' ages, I shouldn't be here at all. How much is it to get them out?"

"They aren't ready yet. They are still getting processed. They did some damage tonight."

"When don't those boys of mine not cost me money?" Jonah muttered.

"If you have a seat, I'll let you know when they are ready for your payment."

Joy glanced around, wondering if she should go wait outside.

Eliana attempted to guide him over to the row of chairs.

"I can do it, woman," Jonah growled.

"Don't you snap at me, Jonah. Stop being so stubborn," Eliana huffed.

Joy's eyebrows rose at Eliana's retort. Jonah snorted and turned, his gaze landing on her. He walked over and took a seat a couple chairs away from Joy, while Eliana sat on his other side.

"Joy," Jonah murmured.

She swallowed hard, unable to believe he was speaking to her.

"Mr. Brooks." Her voice cracked. She peeked back over at the desk to find the deputy ignoring them. He just sat there, typing away at the computer.

How much longer is it going to be to process the guys?

Joy wanted to go ask him, but she had only sat down a few minutes ago when he had told her she'd have to wait.

A look at her watch confirmed it had been seven minutes exactly.

"Heard my boy got into it with your brother," Jonah said, breaking the silence.

Joy nodded. "Yeah."

He blew out a deep breath and ran a hand through his hair. It was the same color as Wade's, but peppered with some gray. He turned his gaze to her, and she was hit with the same colored eyes as Wade.

"Wade tells me you broke it off with him."

Joy froze in shock.

Wade had told his father about them?

"You knew about us?" she asked incredulously.

He held her gaze and jerked his head in a nod. "There isn't anything that goes on at the Blazing Eagle that I don't know about. I saw the difference in my boy. He was happier, and more outgoing. I haven't seen him that genuinely happy in a long time. They think I don't pay attention to them, but I do."

Joy was blown away.

This was the longest conversation she had ever had with the elder Brooks. When she was a child, he would holler at her and her siblings to get off his land.

Joy's heart was pounding away. She sat in disbelief before feeling the spitfire she always had harboring deep inside her come through.

"So let me get this straight. You knew your son was involved with me, but you didn't say anything?" She spun around and glared at him.

"For what? My boys are grown and never listened to me," he snapped. His eyes darkened and narrowed on her. He opened his mouth as if to say something else, but was cut off by Eliana.

"Calm down, Jonah. We don't need your blood pressure up," she murmured, patting the old man's knee.

He nodded and settled back. Wade had shared his amazement about how his father responded to Eliana, and Joy had to admit, she was impressed.

The Jonah Brooks she had grown up knowing was mean, testy, and yelled a lot.

This man next to her had definitely changed.

Joy was at a complete loss. She turned away from Jonah and studied her hands. She had made a huge mistake in putting their families ahead of Wade and her. Thoughts swirled in her mind. If only she could speak with him.

She would apologize.

The first thing she would say? She was an idiot.

Joy bit her lip and thought back to the bar. There had been a blonde standing at Wade's side. Who the hell was she? They had looked really cozy with each other.

It had not even been a week since she had broken it off with him. Had she already been replaced?

"What do you say? You and me?"

There was no way he had replaced her that easily.

Sitting straighter, she realized she was going to have to pull up her big girl panties and talk with Wade again. He had fought her brother twice, wanted her to just think of them only, and she had pushed him away. She'd had trouble believing they could make it work, when all along, he had always had faith in them.

Well, whoever the blonde bitch was, she was going to have to step aside.

Wade Brooks was hers.

"Mr. Brooks." The deputy motioned for Jonah to come to the counter.

Jonah pushed up and walked over to him.

Joy wondered where Lexi was, and why it was taking her so long to come back inside. Joy peeked out the window behind her and saw her sister leaning against the truck on the phone.

Joy tried not to appear as if she was eavesdropping when she heard the policeman mention Wade's name.

"I don't want to alarm you, but Wade must have been really into his cups tonight. His alcohol level was more than four times the legal limit. They've alerted me that he's passed out. They can't get him to wake up, so they have called in an ambulance."

"What?" Jonah roared, slamming his fist down on the counter. "Let me back there. I'll get him to wake up."

Joy's heart skipped a beat. Eliana stood and walked over to Jonah. This time, she didn't say anything, but placed her hand on his back.

What did he mean they couldn't get Wade to wake up? She must have heard him wrong.

"Wait, what did you just say? What's wrong with Wade?" she asked, flying across the room. Getting caught listening to their conversation was the least of her worries. She needed the deputy to repeat what he'd said. Her Wade was fine. It must be someone else with the same first name.

"Let me see my boy," Jonah demanded.

"It's for his safety. They just want to make sure nothing happens to him." The deputy swallowed hard, holding his hands up in the air. "I'm just relaying what the deputies in booking have shared with me."

"An ambulance? Why won't he wake up?" she asked. "What's wrong with him?"

"Ma'am, I'm speaking with Mr. Brooks here about his son—"

"Don't you dismiss me," Joy snapped, her voice ending on a shriek. "I have a right to know what is wrong with Wade."

This was Wade they were talking about. She may have made a mistake regarding their relationship, but she loved him, and no one was going to keep her from him.

"It's all right, Tom. She's Wade's girlfriend," Jonah stated.

Joy almost passed out. Her gaze flew to Jonah's. She must have got knocked on the head during the melee at the bar. Did Jonah just say she was Wade's girlfriend?

The sounds of sirens filled the air.

Her heart pounded, and her lungs burned as she tried to drag fresh air into them.

What was wrong with Wade? Why wouldn't they let his father back there to see him? Panic set in.

She couldn't lose him.

"What is going on?" Lexi rushed back into the station. "There's an ambulance on its way."

The sheriff's station was located on a portion of the highway with nothing else close for miles.

"It's Wade." Joy turned around and burst out crying, unable to finish her sentence.

Lexi immediately wrapped her arms around her and squeezed her tight.

Joy knew he'd seemed off as he turned around when Junior had shouted his name. He was swaying on his feet, and his eyes had been bloodshot. She hadn't been sure if it was the bad lighting or what, but he had looked three sheets to the wind.

She should have done more to keep her brother and Wade from fighting. If she could do it all over again, she would have just walked up to him and demanded he speak with her.

It would have been easy to take him away from the bar and go somewhere they could have talked alone.

Now, Joy just hoped she wasn't too late to tell him how she felt.

25

Wade groaned. He felt as if he had been trampled by a bull. A jackhammer was currently taking up residence in his head, while his mouth felt like he had a million cotton balls stuffed inside of it.

He tried to pry his eyes open, but they were stuck. After several attempts, he finally got them to open. He glanced around the room and took in the stark white walls surrounding him. Bright light floated through the windows to the side of him.

This wasn't the jail cell.

"Where the hell am I?" he mumbled.

His voice didn't even sound like his. It was gritty and raspy. A foul taste lingered in his mouth, and he was desperate for something to take it away.

By the looks of his surroundings, he was in a private hospital room. The clothes he had worn to the festival were no longer on him. They had been replaced by a hospital gown. He was sure they weren't wearable any longer. There had been blood, tears, and rips in them, along with a few questionable fluids.

Wade held up his arm to find an intravenous tube running to a bag with a clear yellow solution.

"Shit," he muttered. This couldn't be good.

There were stickers on his chest connected to a box in the pocket of the gown. He glanced behind him and saw a television screen with squiggly lines and numbers, but didn't know what they stood for. The only one he could make out was the number next to a flashing picture of a heart.

The door opened, and Jonah walked in. His father stood tall, and didn't appear to lean on the cane as much as usual. He shut the door and paused, staring at Wade.

"It would seem the roles have reversed," Jonah said.

Wade snorted and tried to slide up higher. He winced from the pain in his ribs. He remembered Junior's fist landing a body shot. Now that the alcohol had worn off, he felt every one of those hits. His entire body felt as if it had been ran over by a Mac truck.

"How long have I been out?" Wade asked.

"A little over twelve hours." Jonah walked over to the chair that was placed beside the bed and took a seat. "You need something?"

"Water or mouthwash? My mouth tastes like shit."

Jonah hit the call button on the side of the bed. He leaned back and observed Wade.

"You had us worried," Jonah started.

Wade closed his eyes and rested against the pillows. The light was enhancing the elephants stomping around in his head.

"I'm fine. I'm sure I just needed to sleep it off," Wade muttered. Looked like he had got his wish of drinking himself numb to forget Joy.

Before everything had gone black, he'd been sitting in the cell. He, Parker, and Carson had been held together in one cell, while Junior and his friends were in another. Carson and Parker had been joking about the last time the three of them had been locked up together. It had been a few years since they had, and their father had been pissed. Jonah had laid into all three of them, stating they were too old to be in bar brawls and getting arrested.

Well, guess they could say they hadn't learned their lesson.

Wade had been perched on the bench, leaning back against the wall, a large wave of nausea overcoming him while his forehead broke out in sweat.

The room had spun.

The last thing he remembered was hearing his brothers hollering his name.

"You were not fine. Your alcohol level was dangerously high. They had to pump your damn stomach, and the doctors were afraid you were going to seize or go into a coma," Jonah snapped, banging his hand on the bed railing.

"Whatever," Wade mumbled.

Well, now he knew why his mouth tasted the way it did. His body was sore. He was tired, and just wanted to rest. He brought the thin blanket up higher and tried to get comfortable, but it would be practically impossible in this small bed.

"That's why you were sent to the hospital. You started throwing up in the holding cell while unconscious. The damn cops didn't want to have you dying on their watch."

"So it takes something like this to get you to worry about me?" Wade snarled. He opened his eyes and focused on his father. What a fine time for Jonah to start acting like a star parent.

"Don't take that tone of voice with me, boy. I'm still your father, and have always worried about you and your brothers."

"Really?" Wade narrowed his gaze on Jonah. "Where were you when Mom died? We needed you then, but you weren't there. None of us took her death well. We were teenagers who needed our father to help us, and to tell us that everything was going to be all right. But you weren't there, you selfish son of a—"

Wade bit back the rest of what he was going to say when the door opened.

A nurse poked her head inside the room. Her eyes widened, and a small smile fluttered across her face. She was dressed in white scrubs and hot-pink shoes. Her dark brown hair was held back from her face in a low ponytail.

"Oh, you're awake. I'll let the doctors know. Can I get you something?" she asked.

Wade used his free hand to run his fingers through his hair. He didn't even want to know what he looked like. A shower would be great, but with the way his body felt, he would barely be able to stand.

"Can I have something to drink? And a toothbrush?" he asked. The taste in his mouth had to go. His stomach was a little sour, and it wasn't helped by the taste on his tongue.

"Sure." Her face brightened with her smile. "My name is Kat. Just holler if you need something else before I return."

She disappeared back through the door.

Wade stared at the ceiling, not wanting to see his father. Having this conversation while he was in the hospital was not the place, nor the time. Thirty years, and now Jonah wanted to act like he cared or worried about him.

Even when he'd had the heart attack, he'd just

growled and barked, but never stopped to actually say *thank you*.

Wade needed to get out of this damn hospital. He needed to go talk with Joy. He was going to make her see how much he cared for her.

How much he loved her.

He paused.

His heart raced.

Wade searched his heart and knew, without a doubt, that he was in love with Joy.

Nothing was going to keep him from her.

Where was Parker and Carson? Parker was probably seeing to Maddy and Tyler, but where was Carson?

He was going to beat both their asses for leaving Pa with him.

"Hell, I'm sixty years old, and still got to learn how to be a father to you boys," Jonah's voice broke through Wade's thoughts.

He lifted his head and eyed his father. The man sitting next to him looked like Jonah Brooks, sounded like him...

Jonah raised a hand and ran it along his jaw. "If I can quit smoking, I can do better by you and your brothers."

Wade was officially convinced he had died.

Was this an apology from his father for being a crappy parent?

Wade cleared his throat. "Pa, I don't know what to say."

"Well, we have a lot to talk about and clear up between us. It's going to take more than a day, I reckon." Jonah stared down at his hands before turning his attention to Wade.

A knock sounded at the door. It opened, and the same nurse came in, carrying a water pitcher and a little bucket.

"Here's your water and toiletries. If you feel up to it, I can help you get into the bathroom." She tilted the bucket, showing him a toothbrush, mouthwash, and a few things he could use to wash up.

Wade glanced at her. She was a tiny thing. There was no way she'd be able to help him get to the bathroom.

"Where is Parker and Carson?" he asked his father.

"They're down the hall. They've been waiting for you to wake up, Sleeping Beauty," Jonah replied dryly.

Wade turned back to Kat with a smile on his lips. "I'll have my brothers help me up to go to the bathroom."

She nodded and smiled. "Oh, okay."

Another knock sounded at the door, and an older man with graying hair, dressed in a white lab coat, stood at the door. There were a few other people behind him in similar attire.

"So, he has risen," the doctor joked. Walking across the room, he stopped by Wade's bed.

Kat moved out of the way as the small crowd followed him.

"I'm Dr. Brown. How are you feeling?"

Wade took the physician's hand in a solid grip. He bit back a grimace at the stinging from the cuts and bruises on his knuckles.

"Feel like I've been overrun by a stampede of wild bison."

"You look like it too," Dr. Brown chuckled. He glanced over at Jonah. "This is your father?"

"He's my middle boy," Jonah informed him.

"Lucky enough he's as strong as he is. Someone else may not have made it with as much alcohol in his system," Dr. Brown mentioned. He pulled a stethoscope from his jacket pocket and focused on Wade. "Mind if I listen to your lungs?"

Wade shrugged while the doctor leaned over and placed the bell on his chest. Within a few minutes, the doctor finished his assessment.

"Will I live, Doc?" Wade jested. He eyed the physician and the others hovering around his bed.

"You will, as long as you don't drink like that

again." Dr. Brown's smiled disappeared. "You must have had one hell of a party last night."

"I might have had one too many," Wade murmured. He ran a hand over his face and grimaced. Even doing that put a strain on his sore muscles. "When can I get out of here?"

"I'd say later today, if you're up to it. I want you to finish getting those IV fluids. When this bag is done, I want you to get one more. They have some electrolytes to help replace everything you've lost." Dr. Brown folded his arms. "Promise me I won't see you back here again, and I'll make sure I sign your discharge papers so you can leave as soon as the fluids are done."

"Scout's honor." Wade held up his hand.

Dr. Brown nodded, apparently satisfied with what he saw. He stepped forward and held out his hand to Wade again.

"Nice meeting you folks," Dr. Brown said. He gave a nod and motioned for his team to leave.

"I'll keep an eye out for your discharge papers," Kat offered. She waved and disappeared out the door.

Wade reached for the water and took a long sip. It didn't help the taste in his mouth, but his throat was soothed by it.

Jonah stood and walked toward the door.

"Where are you going?" Wade asked.

"Well, I'm sure that girl is going crazy out there in

the waiting room."

Wade's heart jumped.

Joy was here?

He didn't know what he looked like, but if he appeared half as bad as he felt, then he was a mess. The skin around his right eye was swollen. It didn't open completely, leaving him with only a thin slit to see through. His lip was split, and his knuckles were double their normal size.

Jonah paused at the door and glanced over his shoulder. "You do want to see the Whitaker girl, right?"

Wade hesitated and eyed his hands.

"Yeah, you look like shit, but I don't think she is going to care, the way she's been pacing the waiting area."

"Pa, send her in," Wade snapped.

Jonah's eyebrows rose sharply.

"Please." Wade softened his tone.

Jonah nodded and stepped out of the room.

Wade blew out a deep breath and leaned back against the pillows. He closed his eyes and tried to focus on what he would say to Joy when he saw her.

His heart raced just thinking of her.

Right now, all he wanted was to hold her again.

He needed her at his side.

This time, he wasn't letting go.

26

Joy paced the room. She couldn't sit still while waiting on word of Wade. She was going to go crazy if there wasn't some change. She hadn't been permitted to visit him when he was down in the emergency room.

Jonah had been granted permission to go in there with him. They were only letting in the next of kin, because Wade hadn't been the most cooperative patient.

Even unconscious, the man was being too stubborn for his own good.

According to Jonah, Wade had been fighting the staff while they were trying to work on him, forcing them to restrain him.

They had finally gotten him stable, and he was resting comfortably to where they were able to move him to a regular hospital nursing unit.

Joy wrapped her arms around her waist, lost in her

thoughts. She ignored Parker and Carson, who sat quietly in their chairs.

Jonah had left them to check in on Wade. Joy glanced down at her watch. This time, he had been gone too long. Fear and worry consumed her.

Was something else wrong with Wade?

Footsteps caught her attention. She swung around to see Jonah enter the room. Her legs automatically grew weak. Joy reached out and snagged the handle of a chair and sat. Her breaths came fast as she waited for him to update them.

She found Carson's and Parker's eyes locked on their father. Both of their faces were bruised, and their clothes were torn and tattered. They had the look of two brothers who had been in a bar brawl.

If they appeared this bad, she imagined Wade wasn't too far off.

Jonah blew out a sigh and sat in a chair. He propped the cane next to him and looked around.

"He's awake," he announced.

Tears welled up in Joy's eyes. She blinked them back and swiped the few that had escaped, running down her cheeks.

Parker and Carson instantly relaxed.

The room had been tense the last few hours while everyone waited for Wade to open his eyes.

"It's about time," Carson muttered. "Or I was going to go in there and beat his ass until he woke up."

"I think there was enough fighting for one night," Jonah snapped.

"Well, we weren't just going to—"

Jonah held up his hand, shutting Parker up. His face hardened when he faced his boys. Joy sat back, not daring to say one word. She already knew what Parker was insinuating.

It was her brother's fault.

She already knew that.

"It doesn't matter what went down. You boys are getting too old to be in barroom brawls," Jonah said. "What message are you teaching Tyler?"

Parker sat back, his jaw tight. He stood and walked over to the window.

The tension grew. Joy's nerves were getting the best of her. Her leg bounced.

"Your brother is as stubborn as ever. Don't know where he got it from," Jonah snorted.

All eyes in the room landed on Jonah.

He eyed all of them. "What?"

"I knew I should have cut him off," Carson huffed, resting his head in his hands.

Parker walked back over to him and rested a hand on his shoulder. "It's not your fault. He's a grown man trying to drown his pain."

Joy bit her lip and looked away.

Guilt filled her.

Had he been drinking because of her?

Eliana entered with coffees for all the men.

"Here you go," she announced. The older woman walked around and handed out the white cups before taking a seat next to Jonah.

"You sure you didn't want anything?" Eliana asked Joy.

"I'm sure. I'm good, thanks." Joy smiled at her. She wouldn't have been able to drink anything. She was afraid that if she did, she was just going to vomit it up.

She had been so worried about Wade, that her nerves weren't allowing her to eat or drink.

"Joy, I reckon you better go see him first."

Joy's head flew up toward Jonah in shock. She glanced at Carson and Parker, who both nodded in agreement.

"He's not going to want to see us first if he knows you're here," Parker said.

"Are you sure? I mean, I know your family is close." She paused, and three sets of gray eyes landed on her.

Eliana chuckled. "You better go in there, dear."

"Our brother will know we're here. It's you he'll want to see." Caron jerked his head toward the door.

"Okay," she whispered. Joy stood from her chair and nervously brushed her hair from her face as she made her way out of the room. It had been a long night, and she was bone tired.

"He's in room two twenty-four," Jonah said.

She had ridden to the hospital with Jonah and Eliana. Lexi had stayed at the police station to wait for Junior and his friends, as the deputies refused to release them all at the same time. Jonah had paid for his sons, then they'd left to follow the ambulance to the hospital.

The ride had been awkward, but all she kept thinking of was Wade.

Her feet carried her down to the hallway. The hospital unit was busy, with nurses running from room to room. Phones ringing filled the air, while the secretary was busy trying to answer all the calls.

Joy walked past the nurses' station, and continued down the hall until she came upon the room Jonah said was Wade's.

She stood there staring at the door, not knowing what to say.

No time like the present.

Joy knocked gently on the door before pushing it open. She stepped inside to find it was a private room.

Wade laid in the bed with the stark white blankets covering him. There was tubing flowing from his arm to a machine next to the bed. A monitor above had numbers flashing across it.

Fear and emotions she couldn't even describe slammed into her.

What if she had lost him?

A hiccup caught in her throat.

His face was marred with dark-purple bruising. His eyes flew open. The right one barely opened, but his gaze was on her.

"Joy." He cleared his throat and paused. He shifted and grimaced as he pushed himself higher up against the pillows.

She closed the door behind her. Tears blurred her vision. She bit her lip, not sure what to do now that they were staring at each other.

"Wade." Her voice shook. She clenched her hands together, needing to do something with them.

"Come here, baby." Wade opened his arms for her.

Joy flew across the room in a heartbeat.

Wade wrapped his arms around her as the tears flowed freely. Her body was racked with sobs. He just held her, and at the moment, she didn't want to leave his side.

"Why are you crying?" His deep voice rumbled in his chest as he stroked her back.

The scent of him, along with the steady beat of his heart comforted her. Somehow, he had moved over enough to allow her to squeeze in on the small, twin-sized mattress. She was nestled into his side, molding them together perfectly.

Wade used his finger to tip her chin up so he could stare down into her eyes.

"I thought I might have lost you," she whispered. She blinked against the tears that were blurring her vision. Even though his face was covered with bruises, cuts, and was swollen, he was still the sexiest man she had ever seen. Just being this close to him reminded her of everything she felt whenever she was around him.

How had she thought she was better off without him?

She reached up and held his hand, the one holding her face.

Her heart still ached.

Hearing how they couldn't rouse him had had so many scenarios running through her mind.

Wade's thumb ran along her cheek as his gray eyes studied her.

"And that bothered you?" he asked softly.

"Of course it did," she cried out. She pushed him with her hand, wanting to slap him. "I can't lose you."

His hand paused its motions.

"Joy—" He began, but she cut him off.

She'd had a lot of time to contemplate her decision, and now she understood that it was a stupid one. Her family was just going to have to accept that she was in love with Wade.

"I was stupid," she muttered. Sitting up, she wiped her face and took a deep breath. "I thought if we took a break, the fighting between our families would lessen, and we could work on an agreement between them. But being away from you was torture. You were constantly on my mind. I can't resist being with you, Wade."

"Resist being with me?" His eyebrows shot up high.

A laugh escaped her.

"Sounds crazy, doesn't it?"

There was a connection between them. She'd felt as if a piece of her was missing in just the short time they had been apart. When he'd walked away from her, he had taken that section of her heart with him.

He owned her heart.

She was just a shell of herself without him.

It was as if they were meant be, and there was a draw to Wade. Like a moth to a flame, she couldn't stay away.

"No, not at all," he replied. Wade's eyes softened as his hand reached out and took hers, entwining their fingers together. "I've missed seeing your smile, the sound of your laughter, and the feel of you next to me."

He blew out a deep breath and brought her flush against him.

"I've missed your cologne," she admitted, her gaze locked on their hands.

"I've missed feeling this soft skin on mine." He raised her hands up to his lips and pressed a gentle kiss to her skin.

He turned his gray eyes on her, and her core clenched.

Just one look proved that she was his.

"I've missed running my fingers through your hair." Her gaze moved to his thick hair. It was tangled, and stood up all over his head in every direction. "And your voice."

She did.

When he'd whisper in her ear, the rumble of his voice was sure to send a shiver down her spine.

"I've missed hearing you call my name." His crooked grin appeared. He released her hand and took her chin in his hand, pulling her closer to him as he lowered his head to hers.

Joy immediately slid her fingers up his neck and into his thick mop.

She paused, so caught up in his web that she had almost forgotten something that had plagued her.

"Who was that woman at the bar?"

As much as she'd wanted to ask Parker and Carson,

she'd held off. She was going to be woman enough to ask Wade, and no one else.

Wade blinked.

"Stephanie?" Clearing his throat, he slid a hand to the back of her neck. "We dated a few years ago. Yesterday was the first time I'd seen her since we separated. I swear, there is nothing going on with her."

Joy studied his eyes, and deep in her heart, she felt he was telling the truth.

Wade was an honorable man.

He'd never given her a reason not to trust him before.

She nodded, accepting his explanation. "Okay."

"She's not who I've been thinking of every minute of the day." Wade tugged her close to where their lips were a hair's breadth away from each other. "I've missed these soft lips."

A chaste kiss.

She was hooked.

Her gaze dropped down to his lip. It looked excruciating, and she didn't want to be the cause of more agony for him.

"Your lip."

"The pain will be less than you leaving me again."

Joy melted against him. Wade covered her mouth with his in a slow, passionate kiss. She clenched her hands, yanking the strands tight while his tongue took its time dueling with hers.

Wade pulled away from her. Both of them were breathing heavy as they stared at each other.

"Don't leave me again," he said. His hand moved down to her hip and held her to him. "Joy, you are my world. I love you so much. I won't survive if you walk out that door."

Joy froze in place. Fresh tears filled her eyes.

He loved her?

"You love me?" she croaked out.

"This was not the way I had planned to tell you," he admitted. His smile widened. "But, Joy Whitaker, I love you."

She cried out and wrapped her arms around his neck. Sobs racked her as a weight lifted off her shoulders.

"Joy, why are you crying now?" he asked, laughing. He squeezed her tight, and then released her.

Joy dragged in a deep breath, trying to control herself. Her lips spread out into a wide grin.

"Because I'm in love with you, and was scared you wouldn't take me back." She sniffed and wiped the trail of tears away.

She didn't know when she got to be so sappy, but dammit, she was an emotional basket case lately.

"Honey, you've got me. This shit with our families,

we'll figure it out, but we'll do it together. No more making rash decisions without speaking with me first," he said.

"I promise." She giggled. "I just want to be with you."

As long as Wade was by her side, then they would figure out this crazy thing called life.

Wade sat on the steps of his porch with Joy nestled between his legs. The sun was still shining bright, and they were enjoying the beauty of the sun's rays shining across the land.

It was peaceful, with just the two of them. Only the sound of nature surrounded them.

Joy had been a staple in his home since he was discharged from the hospital two days ago.

He had to admit, it felt damn good to have her in his home day and night.

No leaving late at night, or first thing in the morning.

Joy's beauty was the last thing he saw before he went to sleep, and was the first thing he saw when he opened his eyes.

He could get used to it.

His body was sore, and he looked as bad as he felt. The bruises would get worse before they would heal.

It wasn't his first bar fight, but hopefully, it would be the last against Junior Whitaker.

This evening, he was executing a plan.

Something that should have been done years ago.

Joy was unaware of what he had arranged. He glanced down at his watch. They should be arriving any minute.

"I don't understand why we cooked so much food. It's only you and me," Joy said. She turned slightly to glance up at him.

"I'm starving. I told you while you were gone, I couldn't eat. I need to gain back the weight I lost," he teased. He rubbed his washboard stomach. The smells of the food floated out the screen door.

"Boy, please," she muttered, turning back around. She leaned back into his embrace.

He rested his chin on the top of her head and breathed in her scent.

He squeezed her with his legs. "I could get used to you being here all the time."

"Wade, what are you saying?" she asked. This time, she faced him fully.

He shrugged. "Well, you know you don't want to leave, and I don't want you to. Why don't you move in with me?" He wasn't going to beat around the bush. It didn't make sense for her to continue to go back and forth between her parents' house and his.

He had a big enough house for an entire family. She could change whatever she wanted to make it feel like a true home for her.

He just wanted her there.

"That's a big step. Are you sure you're ready for that?"

"I am."

She stood from her perch on the stair and straddled his legs.

He brought her flush against him. "So, what do you say?"

Wade was met with Joy's beautiful smile. Circling her arms around his neck, she leaned in close.

"Well, if you think you can tolerate me around the clock, then yes, I'll move in with you." She pressed a kiss to his lips.

She tried to move away, but he held her close to him, forcing her lips open. He kissed her deeply, excited that they would make his house a home together.

Wheels traveling along the gravel sounded.

They broke apart, breathing hard.

"Who is that?" Joy muttered. She climbed off his lap and sat next to him on the stairs.

Two separate trucks were driving up to his house.

"Company," he replied.

"Wait, is that my dad?" She squinted and held up a hand so she could see.

It was. Wade had called Davis Senior and invited him to his house, as well as his own father.

Tonight, the Whitakers and Brookses were going to have dinner together.

A neighborly dinner.

"And who is in the other truck?" she asked.

Wade pushed off the stairs and stood. "My father."

"Are you crazy?" she asked, standing next to him.

"Nope. We are settling this once and for all." He took her hand in his and brought her close to him. "I spoke to my father, and that story about last year played out differently."

"But how do we know—"

"That's why we are going to make them hash this shit out. If we are going to have a future together, they are going to have to compromise."

Joy bit her lip and eyed the trucks drawing closer to them. "You are crazy, Wade Brooks."

He held her close while they waited.

Jonah had stubbornly demanded to drive his own vehicle, refusing to have Carson bring him.

He parked in front of the attached garage, and Davis pulled in behind him.

Wade glanced down at Joy and squeezed her shoulder.

"It will be okay," he murmured against her head.

Jonah exited his truck first. Reaching inside, he took out his cane.

Joy's father stepped from his truck and closed the door.

Joy's muscles grew tense as the two men turned to each other.

Jonah nodded. "Davis."

"Jonah," Davis replied.

They walked over to where Wade and Joy stood. Tense greetings were shared amongst them.

"Thanks for coming today. I appreciate it," Wade said. "Dinner is ready. Let's go inside where we can eat and chat."

"Something smells good," Jonah muttered. He slowly made his way up the few stairs, with Davis following behind him, and disappeared into the house.

Wade took Joy's hand and pulled her up the stairs. She paused by the door and forced him to turn around.

"Are you sure you know what you're doing?" she asked.

"No, but we are going to go in there and have dinner with our fathers, and see how this plays out."

He leaned down and kissed her softly. Doubt was apparent in her eyes.

"Do you trust me, Joy?"

She nodded.

"Then come on. It's just dinner with two stubborn old men. We can handle them together."

Joy was a nervous wreck. She didn't know how the men sitting at the table could wolf down food like they weren't in the middle of a neighborly war.

The only sound that filled the room was the clinking of silverware against the plates.

"What's wrong, Joy?" her father asked. He looked up from his plate and peeked across the table at her.

Joy put down her fork and glanced at them. All eyes were on her.

"I'm sorry. You're not curious as to why you were invited here?" She was having a hard time believing that Wade had called them over just to eat, and that was it.

Wade chuckled. He took a sip of his iced tea before responding. "Well, since Joy brought it up, I might as well take over." He glanced at them both and leaned back. "There's been tension between our families for years, and it's time it stops. Now."

The room was silent.

Joy was surprised they couldn't hear her heart pounding.

"What are you saying, boy?" Jonah asked.

"I'm saying that this feud between our families is ridiculous. I brought you two here so we can work out a deal so that Joy and I don't have this over our heads." He glanced over at her.

She smiled softly. He was crazy, but she loved him.

She took his hand in hers and turned to face their fathers. "Wade knows how much family means to me, and it's important to him too. We want to be together, but we don't want our families at each other's necks."

Jonah and Davis shared a look.

"You are not leaving until a deal is struck between the two of you," Wade said. "A fair one."

The room grew silent again.

"The land this very house sits on is Whitaker land," Davis began.

Joy stiffened. She didn't know where her father was going with this.

"But seeing how you've made a home for yourself on it, I know it wouldn't make sense to sell this."

Joy couldn't relax. When they'd heard Wade had built his house on their former land, her father had just about lost his mind.

"In my anger, I may have fibbed slightly to your brother last year." Her father glanced at her before turning back to Jonah. "It would seem something I said in anger got my son riled up, so I feel somewhat responsible for it. Not that Junior isn't fully responsible for his part, but I do want to apologize."

Joy's mouth dropped open.

"Well, we have all said and done things we didn't mean to in anger. We can't tell what the future holds," Jonah noted, "but the offer I made to you last year still stands. It's not the exact land, but it is comparable. It's plush, and would be good for sheep."

Joy peered at Wade, and he nodded. Were the two stubborn men about to strike a deal?

Davis stared at Jonah for a moment, then held out his hand. Jonah took it in a firm shake.

"You have yourself a deal," Davis said.

Tears welled up in Joy's eyes. Was the feud finally over?

"I'll call my lawyer on Monday and have him draw up the contract," Jonah offered.

"That would be perfect," Davis replied. Picking up his fork, he dug back into his food. "This pot roast is so tender."

Joy sat in awe.

That was it?

"Close your mouth, honey. Don't wanna catch any flies," her father said.

Joy hesitantly took a bite. It was unbelievable that everything was over, just like that.

"So, I hear that oldest boy of yours is getting married soon," Davis said.

"That he is," Jonah replied. "Got another grand-baby on the way too."

Joy's eyebrows jumped up. Was that a hint of pride in Jonah's voice?

A smile formed on her face. Maybe Wade was right. The older generation could learn something from them by breaking bread together.

Wade pushed back his chair and stood, removing her fork from her hand.

"What are you doing?" She laughed. She finished chewing, and almost choked on her food as she watched him kneel down beside her.

He twisted her chair around so she could face him. His crooked grin appeared. Even with the bruising, he was still devilishly handsome.

"Joy Whitaker..."

Her gaze dropped down to the velvet box that had somehow appeared in his hand.

"Oh my God," she breathed.

Wade took her hand in his. Butterflies appeared in her stomach, and she waited for him to continue.

She peered at their fathers, who leaned back with pleased looks on their faces.

"You are the light of my life, and I can't see myself without you. I need you by my side always. You mean the world to me, and I just have to ask..." He paused and opened up the box, displaying the massive diamond ring nestled inside.

"Wade..." Her voice ended on a hitch.

"Joy, will you marry me?"

"Yes, Wade. Yes, I will marry you," she cried out. The tears spilled out and ran down her face.

He took the ring from the box and slid it on her finger.

She leaned forward and pressed her lips to his, sealing the promise to love him forever.

She pulled back and gazed down at the flawless ring. It was a perfect fit, and it was going to take some getting used to, having something this heavy on her finger.

Glancing at her father, she had to ask, "Did you know about this?"

Her father smiled. "Yes, baby. Wade came over to the house yesterday. We had a long conversation, and I certainly approve."

Wade stood from where he was kneeling and helped her to her feet. "I wasn't taking any chances, and wanted to do this right. If we are going to have a future together, then I wanted to do the honorable thing and ask for your father for your hand."

Her heart fluttered at the lengths he was willing to go to, to ensure they got started off on the right foot.

He laughed, wiping her cheeks with his hands. "Why the tears?"

"I don't know. This is all so much, but I'm just so happy."

Wade wrapped his arms around her, and she never wanted to leave them.

He was just too sneaky.

She figured he was testing the waters by asking her to move in with him earlier.

But that was okay.

She was right where she belonged, and had no plans of ever leaving again.

EPILOGUE

The sun beat down on Wade's back as he ran along the yard.

He cut left, trying to get away from Carson. He spun in a different direction, and the football landed right in his hands.

"Yes!" Tyler hollered.

"Son of a bitch," Carson cursed, laughing.

Wade held his hands up in the air with the football tight in his grasp. He jogged to their makeshift end zone.

"Touchdown," he announced.

They were playing a friendly game of touch football with Tyler, and just having some fun.

Maddy and Joy sat on the back porch watching them.

"You're getting slow, old man," Wade teased Parker.

"It's the knee." Parker's limp was more exaggerated.

Wade chuckled, walking back to his nephew. "I'm calling bullshit. Hell of a throw."

He held up his hand, and Tyler jumped up, returning the high five.

It had been a month since Wade had proposed to Joy. She had moved in that night, and they hadn't looked back. They were in no rush to start planning the wedding, since Parker and Maddy were about to jump the broom.

"Are you strong men ready for lunch?" Maddy called out.

She and Joy came down the stairs.

"I'm starving, Mom," Tyler said.

"When aren't you starving, little boy?" Maddy snorted.

Wade followed behind Tyler to where Maddy and Joy were headed.

Wade had eyes only for Joy. Her hips swung slowly as she strolled alongside Maddy.

He couldn't push aside the memories of that morning when she'd climaxed while riding him. The pure look of ecstasy on her face was something he couldn't wait to see again.

Her moving in with him was the best thing. They were learning more about each other, and Wade didn't think he could fall any more in love with her.

Since the night of the truce, their fathers had carried out the deal that had been struck.

The land Jonah offered had officially switched hands, and was now Whitaker property.

Wade was impressed with how much his father had changed. He was stronger, and no longer walked with the cane.

Even Joy's parents were starting to accept their relationship. Lexi had already been to their house a few times, helping Joy decide on some changes she wanted to make.

It was now their home.

Junior hadn't really come around, and Wade frankly didn't care if he did or not.

As long as Joy was happy, that was all that mattered.

Now, if Junior was a reason for her tears, then Wade would have to have another chat with her brother.

"What do we have here?" Wade murmured.

"Um, y'all need to go wash your hands," Joy announced, pointing over to the patio's sink.

Wade was impressed by his brother's patio. He had renovated it to include an outdoor kitchen, along with a large grill, sink, and prep area. A fridge was located under the counters. It was giving him some ideas of what they could do with their home.

"Do we have to?" Tyler asked, looking at his hands. "Mine look clean."

"Tyler Brooks!" Maddy stomped her feet. Her small belly was more pronounced, and Wade couldn't wait to meet his future niece, or nephew.

"Come on, little man." Carson slapped Tyler on his shoulder and guided him over to the sink. "There are some things you just don't argue with women. Keep that in mind."

Wade laughed. He had to agree.

"Picked a date yet?" Parker asked, coming to stand next to him, while Carson and Tyler went first at the sink.

"Not yet. There's no rush." Wade grinned. He was still in awe that Joy had agreed to marry him. Each morning, he just stared at her as she slept.

There was something about seeing his ring on her finger he couldn't even begin to explain.

Parker chuckled. "I hear you."

"Maybe next summer."

He glanced over and watched Maddy and Joy work together to put the food out on the table. Carson and Tyler took their seats, and his gaze landed on Maddy's stomach. He was suddenly hit with a small twinge of jealousy.

One step at a time.

He turned back and ran his hands underneath the water.

The sound of someone gagging drew his attention. Joy was bent over at the edge of the patio with her hands braced on her knees.

The contents of her stomach hit the ground.

"Are you okay?" Maddy asked her.

Wade rushed over to her, wiping his hands on the back of his jeans as he arrived at her side.

Resting his hand on her back, he asked, "You all right, babe?"

She lifted her head and straightened. "I think so." She grimaced and shook her head. "I don't know what came over me."

"Was it something you ate?" he asked, holding her close.

"No, I don't think so." She blew out a deep breath.

Maddy stood by, looking concerned. "We have some ginger ale in the fridge. I'll grab you one."

When Joy nodded, Maddy spun around and jogged away.

"Do you want to go home?" Wade asked.

She didn't look well at the moment, and he was

worried. He could have her at the hospital in under an hour if he needed to.

"No, I'm sure it will calm down." She smiled softly, and leaned her head against his chest.

He kissed the top of her head. "Just say the word and we'll go straight home." He rubbed her back gently in soothing circles. He wasn't sure who he was trying to comfort, though, her or him?

"Here you go." Maddy appeared with the soda in her hand.

"Thank you." Joy stepped back, away from Wade, and took the can from her. She popped it open and took swig from it.

Maddy eyed Joy with a small smile before she went back to the table with the others.

"Better?" Wade asked. He watched her close her eyes and breathe in before blowing the air out.

"I just hope it doesn't keep happening." She moved closer to him and played with his T-shirt.

"Why would it happen again?" Did he need to take her to the hospital? Was something wrong with her?

"Hopefully, it won't last for the next six months." She paused and glanced up at him.

"Six months?" Wade swallowed. He ran a hand along his face, unable to believe what he was hearing. "Are you serious?"

She giggled. "I was planning to tell you tonight

after dinner, but apparently, this baby is wanting you to know now."

Wade whooped and scooped her up in his arms. He swung her around, unable to contain his excitement.

"What the hell is going on?" Carson called out.

"We're having a baby!" Wade hollered back, holding Joy up in the air.

His brothers, Maddy, and Tyler, all cheered and clapped.

Joy laughed, swinging her feet. "Wade, put me down!"

He set her on her feet and took her face in his hands. He pressed a hard kiss to her lips.

"I love you, Joy."

"I love you too, Wade. I'm so happy right now, I don't even know what to do." Joy gripped his shirt in her hands with a wide grin on her lips.

"Well, Whitaker, when we get home, I'm sure I can come up with a few things we can do," he joked.

"I look forward to it, Brooks."

Wade covered her lips with his. He couldn't wait to get his woman home so he could show her just how happy her news had made him.

A NOTE FROM THE AUTHOR

Dear reader,

Thank you for taking the time to read Roping a Cowboy. This is book two in the Blazing Eagle Ranch and I'm having fun with these cowboys. Writing Wade and Joy's story was so much fun. These two are meant for each other.

I need to know if you want me to keep going with this series, so that means I have to hear from you. If you don't know what to say, just say, "Peyton, I need Carson's book!"

Warm wishes,
Peyton Banks

Knockin' the Boots

She was his best friend's sister and should have been off-limits.

Rashad Mays was a ranch hand on the Blazing Eagle Ranch. He had grown up in Shady Springs and had no intention of leaving. This was his home, and he was ready to settle down. Only the woman that captured his eye was the sister of his best friend, Nate.

There were unspoken rules between friends when it came to their little sisters--don't touch.

Yani Polk was not like other women. She didn't chase after cowboys for a casual roll in the hay. She was a lady. Sexy, curvy, successful, and currently the star of his late-night fantasies.

He'd thought he would be able to push her out of

BLAZING EAGLE RANCH NOVELLA

his mind, but when she came strolling onto the ranch, he couldn't resist. Her smile and the gentle sway of her hips called to him.

The sizzling attraction was too great to resist. Rashad did the unthinkable. He broke the rules.

Yani was the woman for him, and he was willing to fight to prove it.

You can find Knockin' the Boots in Cowboys for a Cause, a western romance anthology benefiting COVID-19 relief.

Order Cowboys for a Cause now! Click HERE to grab your copy!

ABOUT THE AUTHOR

Peyton Banks is the alter ego of a city girl who is a romantic at heart. Her mornings consist of coffee and daydreaming up the next steamy romance book ideas. She loves spinning romantic tales of hot alpha males and the women they love. Make sure you check her out!

Sign up for Peyton's Newsletter to find out the latest releases, giveaways and news!
Newsletter:
bit.ly/2PcR6io

Want to know the latest about Peyton Banks? Follow her online!
Twitter:
twitter.com/the_PeytonBanks

Facebook:
www.facebook.com/PeytonBanksAuthor

Amazon page:

www.amazon.com/-/e/B073SK6SLC

Goodreads:
www.goodreads.com/peytonbanks

Bookbub:
www.bookbub.com/authors/peyton-banks

Instagram:
instagram.com/peytonbanks_author

Pieces of Me

Hard Love

Retain Me

Silent Deception

Charity Anthology

Cowboys for a Cause

Tempt Me: A Romance Limited Edition Collection

Love Me Always

Mafia Romance Series

Unexpected Allies (The Tokhan Bratva 1)

Unexpected Chaos (The Tokhan Bratva 2) TBD

Unexpected Hero (The Tokhan Bratva 3) TBD